Round Up

Book 3 Cowboy Code Series

Lauren Fraser

Blurb

Why settle for one cowboy when you can have two?

Sometimes a girl just needs to escape from real life, hide-out and regroup. And what better place than a ranch surrounded by sexy cowboys? After all, what's an escape without a little daydreaming?

Fleeing from a relationship gone wrong, Julia Cragan needs to reassess her life, and learn to trust men again. Befriending two gay, sexy cowboys seems like a safe choice. Fantasy without the
reality.

Wait... are they a couple?

Best friends Kasey Davison and Duncan Kane live together, work together and play together. They never imagined they'd find a woman who fit with them longer than one night. Until Julia.

In her cozy little bubble with Kasey and Duncan, Julia finally feels safe, accepted, and desired. But eventually, you have to get back to the real world. Or maybe you don't.

**This is a stand-alone book that is part of the Cowboy Code Series. **

Contents

Chapter One

What the hell was going on?

Kasey Davison watched the cab pull to a stop in front of the ranch house. A skinny woman with long, light brown hair slid out of the backseat. She stared up at the house while the driver pulled out her suitcase from the trunk and then drove away, leaving the woman standing alone.

Shit, so much for getting his work done. He pulled off his gloves and tossed them on the side of the wheelbarrow. As he approached the woman, he examined her from head to toe. She was attractive. A little on the skinny side for his liking, but overall, not bad. He took in the heeled boots, expensive looking jeans, and fancy purse and snorted. Definitely out of place on a dusty ranch.

"Can I help you?" he asked.

The woman looked up at the house again and chewed her full bottom lip. "Umm, I'm looking for Katherine McCray."

"She's not here."

"Do you know when she'll be back?"

"As a matter of fact, I do. She'll be back in about ten days."

Her shoulders sagged. "Ten days?" The woman looked defeated as she eyed the bag on the ground beside her. "Great," she muttered.

"There something I can help you with?"

"No, thanks." She grabbed the handle of her bag and turned towards the driveway. The wheels of the suitcase caught in on a rock and the bag tipped slightly before she could right it. Her head dropped forward, and she audibly sighed, then turned around. "Actually, can I borrow your phone to call the cab back? Mine died yesterday, and I haven't had a chance to charge it."

Kasey crossed his arms over his chest and stared at the woman. Who was this woman and what kind of person showed up unannounced and had the cab drop them off?

"Mind my asking why you're looking for Kat?"

"She still goes by Kat?" She smiled.

"Yep. So how do you know her?"

"We're friends."

Considering he'd never seen her before, they couldn't be that close of friends. She sure as hell hadn't been at the wedding. "Close are ya'?"

She chewed her bottom lip again and her eyes welled up. "We used to be. I haven't seen her in a while."

The way she stood there wringing her hands together all slouched into herself reminded him of a scared animal. His stomach knotted as he looked at her. *Shit, maybe he could ease up a bit.* "I'm Kasey and you are?"

"Oh, umm, I'm Julia." She glanced up at him beneath her lashes and flashed him a tight smile. He'd never seen lashes that long before. Kat always put a bunch of crap on her eyes to make her lashes look that long, but this woman didn't appear to have a lick of makeup on.

His gut clenched as checked out the fresh-faced newcomer. Shit, if she put makeup on, she'd be a knockout.

"So, Julia, you and Kat used to be friends?"

"Yeah, we grew up together." She sighed. "We sort of lost touch over the years."

"And yet here you are, showing up on her doorstep with a suitcase?"

She snorted. "If you knew me, it wouldn't seem so strange."

He widened his stance and stared down at her. "Well, I don't know you, and it strikes me as more than a little odd."

Julia looked down at her shoes. "I'm sure it does. So, about that phone, can I borrow yours."

Just as he was reaching into his pocket, Duncan called out for him. "Kase?"

"Yeah, I'm out front," he yelled back.

Duncan rounded the corner. He sauntered towards them with that cocky swagger of his that Kasey liked so much. Even after all this time, he still enjoyed watching him walk. Duncan glanced towards the woman and grinned. "Well, hello there."

Julia blushed. "Hi," she murmured.

Duncan waggled his eyebrows and winked at him. The man never changed. Put an attractive woman in front of him and he couldn't seem to help himself from flirting.

"This is an 'old friend' of Kat's." Kasey air-quoted the 'old friend'. He still wasn't entirely sure what to think about this stranger showing up when Kat was away, claiming to be her friend.

"Oh yeah. So how come you weren't invited to the wedding?" Duncan asked.

"Kat got married?" she asked, her green eyes sparkled with joy.

"Sure did. She's away on her honeymoon right now?" Duncan told her.

"That explains why she's gone for ten days then." She gripped the handle of her suitcase again. "I guess I'll just get out of your way, then."

"Hang on." Duncan reached out and grabbed her arm. She flinched back.

He held out his hands, palms forward. "It's okay. I'm not going to hurt you."

"I didn't think you were," she said belligerently.

Kasey met Duncan's eyes. What was going on here?

"Look, if you're friends with Kat, we aren't just going to send you off without a place to go," Duncan said.

"We're not?" Kasey asked.

"No, we're not." Dunc glared at him.

"What are you going to do, then?" Julia asked.

Duncan shrugged. "We'll call her."

"You're going to call her on her honeymoon?" Julia's voice rose high in outrage.

"Sure, why not?"

"Because it's her honeymoon," she argued. Her eyes widened as if they were crazy for even suggesting something like that.

Duncan shrugged. "Clearly you don't know her husband. Justin is a control freak. He needs a daily check-in anyway, so he won't be too pissed if I call."

Julia warily eyed Duncan, then looked over at Kasey as if she wanted confirmation. He sighed. "It's fine."

Since Kasey still had his phone in his hand, he dialed. Justin answered and growled. "This better be good."

"Did I get you at a bad time?"

"It's my honeymoon. What do you think?"

"I think you're the one who wanted to check-in daily, dude."

"Yeah, but in case you forgot, I'm supposed to call you. So, what's up? Why the phone call?"

"Umm, is Kat available?"

"Kat?"

"Mmm hmm."

"Why do you want to talk to her?"

He sighed. "Just put her on."

"Fine," Justin grumbled.

While he waited for Kat to come to the phone, he looked at Julia, watching him avidly. She appeared relaxed, and not at all worried about how the conversation was going to go. She didn't look like she had anything to hide, but her whole behavior was a little on the weird side.

"Hello."

"Hi darlin', sorry to interrupt the honeymoon, but a friend of yours just showed up at the ranch."

"A friend of mine? Who?"

"She says her name is Julia."

"Julia? Julia Cragan?"

"I don't know," Kasey responded. He looked at the woman in question. "What's your last name?"

"Cragan."

"That's her," he told Kat.

"Oh my god, really?" Kat squealed. "How does she look?"

Typical woman. Not any kind of wondering why she showed up unannounced. No. How does she look? "I don't know. I've never seen her before," he grouched.

"Fine," she huffed. "Let me talk to her."

He looked at Julia and held out the phone. "She wants to talk to you."

She grabbed it from him and quietly began speaking. She walked a few feet away from them as she talked. Her voice pitched low so he couldn't make out what she was saying.

"So, what do you think?" Duncan asked.

"Weird."

Dunc smirked. "I meant, what do you think of her?"

Kasey eyed the other woman, the way her jeans clung to a surprisingly shapely ass. Her light brown hair hung past the middle of her back. She was definitely attractive, in a girl next door kind of way. But the way she had flinched when Duncan touched her was really what drew him in. There was a story there, he was sure. And he intended to find out what it was.

The woman in question walked back and handed the phone to Kasey. "Kat wants to talk to you," she said.

"Hey, Kat," he said.

"Julia is going to stay at the ranch until we get back from our honeymoon," Kat told him.

"Okay, is she sleeping in the main house, or do you want her to bunk with us?" he asked.

"Umm, probably the main house. She sounds off, like something is up with her and I would rather she didn't feel all invaded and scrutinized in case there's more to the story than she let on right now." Kat paused. "How does she look, not like is she pretty, that I already know, but like, how does she seem? You're good at reading people, so what's your take?"

Kasey looked over at the woman in question. Julia pulled her sleeves down over her hands and chewed her bottom lip as she watched him. She didn't have the outward confidence a beautiful woman in designer clothes would normally have. She reminded him of a wounded bird.

Conscious of his audience, Kasey replied. "Running, I think, but we'll get it sorted out. We'll take care of your friend for you until you get back. Tell Justin we have everything under control, and he can consider this his call for the day, so he's all yours."

Kat chuckled. "I'm sure he'll be happy to hear that."

If Kasey knew Justin, he could just imagine what he had on the agenda for today, so having uninterrupted time with Kat would definitely be appreciated. "Enjoy the rest of your day," he said as he hung up the phone.

He pocketed his phone and made eye contact with Duncan before turning to their guest. "So, it looks like you are bunking with us for the next 10 days."

Her eyes boggled, and she took a step away from him. "With you? What? No, I can't bunk with you," she stammered.

"Sorry, not with us, but here at the ranch with us. We'll put you in Kat and Justin's place until they get back. Then, if you are still here when they get home, we can figure something else out."

Duncan nodded his head. "Alright, follow me." He reached for her suitcase.

"I can get it," she murmured.

"I'm sure you can, but my mama would smack me upside the head if she knew I didn't carry your suitcase for you," he said with a wink.

Julia lowered her eyes and blushed again.

Kasey noted the slight wince on her face as she took a step onto the porch step. "You okay?"

"Yeah, just tweaked my knee the other day. It's nothing."

"If you're sure," he said.

She nodded. "Don't worry about me."

Duncan pushed open the front door of the ranch house. "Let me give you the nickel tour." He gestured to the right. "Living room, then through here is the kitchen."

"Wow," Julia sighed as she scanned the large open-concept family-space.

"Dee really liked to cook, so when Justin did the renovations, they went a little over the top," Duncan said.

"Dee?" Julia asked.

"Justin's sister. She used to live here until a few months ago, when she moved in with her boyfriend, Brody. She's around here a lot though, so you'll see her pretty regularly," Duncan told her.

They continued their tour down the hall. "Guest bathroom is here." Duncan pushed open the bathroom door and continued down the hall. He opened the door to Denise's old bedroom. Since it was the second largest bedroom in the house, it made the most sense to put her in there for the time being. "This is where you'll sleep."

"Wow, this is all really nice," Julia said as she ran her hand over the fluffy, pale pink duvet cover.

Kasey scanned the bedroom. It looked like a bedroom to him, but then he wasn't into design and all that crap like Denise and Kat seemed to be. Give him a comfy bed and he couldn't care less about anything else.

Duncan placed her suitcase in the corner of the room. "Why don't we go into the family room and get better acquainted."

"Umm, I'm kind of tired," Julia said, looking down at the floor.

"I'm sure you are, darlin'. We won't take up too much of your time. We'll get you something to eat. You look like you could use some fuel," Duncan said.

She glanced up at him warily. "Umm, I can probably forage around and find myself something."

"Look, I don't want to be a jerk, but we don't know you and unfortunately, with them gone, we oversee the ranch. So, even though Kat vouched for you, we need to get to know you a bit before we just leave you in their house," Kasey told her.

Duncan looked over and glared. "What the fuck?" he mouthed.

Kasey shrugged. Sure, she looked harmless, but they didn't know this woman at all. Kat had a big heart and would do anything for the people she cared about, but she had been taken advantage of before by so-called friends back in New York. He didn't want that to happen again. Julia might be completely nice, but there was something going on with her. He just didn't have a clue what it might be.

Julia sighed. "Fine." She turned and walked out of the bedroom.

Duncan gave him a puzzled look. "What's up?"

"I don't know, call it a feeling, but there's more to her than meets the eye," Kasey said.

"Okay, you're usually right about these things, so I'll trust your gut, but be nice. You're coming off a little scary," Duncan said. He smacked Kasey on the ass as he walked out of the room.

"Shit," Kasey muttered to himself. He knew his size was intimidating to people. Normally, being 220 pounds of muscle was a good thing. Apparently, this wasn't one of those times. But there wasn't much he could do about it. He rolled his shoulders and shook out his arms to relax in the hopes it made a difference before he followed Julia and Duncan into the kitchen.

"Have a seat," Duncan told Julia as he indicated the stools around the island. Julia slid onto the stool furthest away from the men and pulled her sleeves down over her hands.

Kasey had noticed the nervous gesture before. Was it nerves or guilt that made her look so anxious? He was going to find out before he'd leave her alone in Justin and Kat's house.

"Let's see what we can dig up to eat. Kase, maybe you could make some coffee," Duncan said.

Shit, clearly, he was still giving off an asshole vibe, judging by the look Duncan just gave him.

"I'm on it." He rounded the quartz counter and started making coffee, glancing at Julia periodically as he did. She was definitely skittish, but people didn't normally just show up at someone's house out of the blue without a reason.

Duncan pulled ingredients out of the fridge and placed them on the counter. "Sandwiches, okay? I'm not much of a cook."

Kasey snorted. That was putting it mildly.

Duncan scowled. "It's not like you are any better."

"Umm... I can make something," Julia said quietly.

"You can cook?" Kasey asked.

She shrugged. "I used to be a chef."

"Damn, now we're talking." Duncan grinned. "By all means, please, make yourself at home," he said as he gestured to the spread of food he'd dumped on the island.

Julia walked over to the sink and washed her hands, then took a visibly deep breath before turning around to face the men.

Kasey glanced at Duncan. The puzzled look he shot him said he'd noticed the fortifying breath Julia had taken as well. What was her story?

Julia pulled containers out of the fridge and began spooning various ingredients into a bowl.

"So, you said you used to be a chef. What do you do now for work?" Kasey enquired.

"I haven't been working. My partner..." she paused. "His schedule made me working challenging."

"How so? Do you have kids?" Kasey asked.

"Thank god no," she replied.

"So why couldn't you work?" Kasey pressed.

Duncan laughed. "Sorry about the third degree. We don't get a lot of beautiful women out here on the ranch, so he's a bit out of practice on the conversation skills."

Julia smiled at Duncan. "No problem. I'd be curious about someone just showing up, too." She glanced at Kasey and gave him a small smile.

Shit, now he felt like an asshole. "Sorry," he muttered, "I wasn't trying to be rude. I'm just trying to figure out what brought you here."

Julia spread the concoction she had made on thick slices of bread. She examined the various bags of cold cuts, then began layering meat and vegetables on the sandwich. "Understandable," she replied.

She scooped an avocado out of the bowl on the island and began cutting it open. "My boyfriend and I broke up and..." She paused. "I didn't know where else to go."

"You didn't have friends where you were living you could have stayed with?" Duncan asked.

"It's complicated," Julia quietly replied. She took a deep breath, then raised her head. She pushed plates towards Kasey and Duncan.

Kasey eyed the sandwich in front of him. How the hell had she made a sandwich that looked like that out of what they had? It looked like something out of a magazine. "Wow, this looks amazing," he said.

Julia blushed at the compliment and dropped her gaze down to the island.

Weird. You'd think a chef would be used to compliments.

Duncan took a large bite of his sandwich. "Holy shit, what did you put in here? This is freaking amazing."

Julia laughed. "Nothing special, it's just a homemade spicy sandwich spread I put on. It gives a little kick."

"It's freaking amazing," Duncan told her.

"Thanks." Julia smiled at Duncan.

When she turned towards Kasey, the pleasure from Duncan's compliments still brightened her face. Who was he kidding? She didn't need makeup to make her a knockout, she just needed to smile. Shit, the woman was gorgeous. The punch to the gut of sexual awareness took him by surprise, given how suspicious he was of her.

Kasey cleared his throat. "Where were you living before you came here?"

"California," Julia replied.

"And you just hoped on a plane to Arizona without calling Kat first?" Kasey asked.

"I left a message for her when I was at the airport." Tears welled up in Julia's eyes and she dropped her head into her hands. "God, this so embarrassing," she whispered.

Kasey looked at Duncan in confusion and he shrugged.

"What's embarrassing?" Duncan asked.

"You must think I'm so pathetic, just showing up here." She sniffed. "And you aren't wrong. I mean, what kind of twenty-eight-year-old woman has nowhere else to go except the home of her childhood best friend?" She dropped her face in her hands and rested her elbows against the island. Sobs wracked her body.

God, he hated when a woman cried. The anguish in her voice tore through him. He didn't even know this woman, and he wanted to hold her and take the pain away. He looked at Duncan. His face stricken with the same torment Kasey was feeling.

Kasey pushed off his stool and walked over to Julia. She flinched when he touched her shoulder. He soothed her like he would an injured animal. Whispering softly to her, until finally, she turned into his arms and allowed him to comfort her.

Her body sagged against him. Kasey leaned against the counter and absorbed her weight. He stroked her hair and met Duncan's gaze over the top of her head. Duncan winced as he looked at Julia.

After several moments, the tears seemed to ease up a bit, and a shudder rippled through Julia's body. She took a deep breath and released her hold on Kasey's shirt.

She rubbed her face with her hands and wiped away the tears. She fingered Kasey's wet shirt. "Sorry about that," she murmured.

Kasey glanced down at his shirt. "No problem, it'll dry." He tipped her chin up with his finger. "You want to talk about it? We're good listeners."

"After that little breakdown, I probably owe you some kind of explanation," Julia said.

"You don't owe anyone shit," Duncan replied. "If you want to tell us, we'd love to hear. If you don't, that's your right too."

As much as Kasey was dying to know what her history was, he knew Duncan was right. He would hate to have someone prying into his private life. Hell, he didn't even talk to his family about most of the things in his life and he loved them, let alone telling virtual strangers about his life. "Duncan's right, whatever you feel like sharing is up to you."

Julia flashed a sad smile. Her bottom lip trembled. "I appreciate that." She grabbed a paper towel off the roll on the counter and blew her nose. "I can't even imagine what you both must think of me. I promise I'm not some head case. I just..."

She sighed. "Let's just say I realized how unsafe my relationship was. I left quickly while he was at work and only took a few things with me."

She pushed her hair off her forehead and tucked it behind her left ear. Tears welled in her eyes again as she looked at them. She blinked and a lone tear slid down her cheek, and she angrily brushed it away. "I hate that it's come to this. I hate that I haven't seen Kat in years and when I show up, it's like this." She waved her hand angrily and growled. "I'm not normally this big of a train wreck."

"You aren't a train wreck. You're obviously leaving a shitty situation. I'm glad you had someplace to go," Duncan told her as he reached out and squeezed her hand.

"Do we need to worry about this guy coming after you?"

Julia shook her head. "Tyler doesn't know anything about Kat."

"Good enough." Duncan nodded.

"Do you happen to have a picture of the guy just in case, so we know what he looks like?" Kasey asked.

"He won't come here. Even if he knew where I was, that's not his style," Julia told them.

"It doesn't hurt to err on the side of caution," Kasey replied.

"I guess you're probably right." Julia exhaled audibly, then pulled her phone from her purse. She pressed the power button. "Shoot, sorry I forgot; I need to charge it."

Kasey scooped the phone from the island and plugged it in to the charger on the kitchen counter. He turned back and smiled at Julia. "It'll be ready in no time."

He made eye contact with Duncan, then looked back at Julia. The woman was spent. Exhaustion was evident in every piece of her body. "Why don't we let you get some rest. We are around, working near the house today, so if you need anything, just give a holler."

Duncan grabbed a pad of paper and pen from the drawer. "I wrote down our cell phone numbers so you can call if you need anything. We'll check in on you later to see how you are settling in."

"Thank you both," Julia said. "I'm just going to go crawl in bed. I won't be such a hot mess when you see me tomorrow."

Kasey took one last look at Julia, then turned on his heel and made his way towards the front door. With his hand on the handle, he turned back around. "You have the house to yourself. We'll tell the guys not to come in for food for the next couple of days. We live in the big cabin just on the other side of the barn. You can't miss it."

"Ok, thank you." Julia nodded.

Kasey didn't want to leave her. He didn't even know her, but the idea of leaving her alone, sad and upset, nearly gutted him. Duncan placed a hand on his shoulder. "Let's give her some space," Duncan whispered.

Kasey nodded. "We'll see you later," he called out as he opened the door. He took a deep breath of air when he stepped outside.

"Jesus, that sucked," Duncan muttered as soon as he closed the door behind them.

"That's putting it mildly," Kasey replied.

"Guess that explains why she reminded me of Chester," Duncan mumbled as he looked back towards the front door.

Kasey grimaced as he thought of the abused horse Dee had adopted. The thing had been starved and beaten within an inch of his life. Tied to a post and left for dead. The animal had tried to break free and nearly cut off his own head with the amount of pulling he had done on the chain around his neck. It had embedded the chain in his neck so deeply the vet had to perform surgery to remove it.

Even now, Kasey could still picture the whip marks that had covered the animal's entire body when he had arrived. It had taken weeks for the horse to let any of them close to him. Now, whenever Dee was in the yard, he followed her around like a lovesick puppy. Chester was fine now, but it took a lot of work for him to trust anyone again. Kasey hoped it wouldn't be the same for Kat's friend.

"What kind of guy abuses a woman?" Duncan asked.

Kasey thought about some of the assholes in his hometown. "Unfortunately, it's more common than we'd like."

"Freakin' pussies every last one of them," Duncan growled.

Kasey nodded in agreement. He cupped the back of Duncan's neck and squeezed it. "Let's get back to work. You can take some of that aggression out on the fence posts."

"Yee haw, let the good times begin," Duncan grumbled.

"If you still need to expend some energy after that, I'm sure we can come up with something else to take our minds off things," Kasey told him.

The air between them shifted as Duncan looked at Kasey. His gaze trailed down Kasey's body and lingered near his belt buckle. Duncan licked his lips, and Kasey's cock twitched to life. "Or we could go back to our place, and I could fuck you raw and burn off some energy that way," Duncan told him. His blue eyes darkened with arousal as he stared at Kasey.

He stepped towards Duncan. He loved how Duncan went from zero to aroused in a heartbeat whenever Kasey was interested. They'd fucked out a lot of emotion over the years they'd been friends. Hell, that was how they crossed the line from friends to lovers in the first place. Some asshole and his friends had picked a fight with Kasey in a bar after a rodeo competition and Duncan, being the good friend, had jumped in to even out the numbers. The adrenaline that had been surging through them after the fight had been channeled into fucking each other. Kasey had never even thought about kissing a guy before that, let alone fucking one. The entire night had been eye opening, to say the least, and they'd been whatever they were to each other ever since.

"As good as that sounds, we need to get those posts dug, but I'm open for cutting out early if you are," Kasey told him.

"Aren't I in charge when Justin isn't here?" Duncan asked, as he stepped closer to Kasey.

Kasey chuckled. "You like when I make you work for it." He winked and walked towards the barn. If his jeans fit a bit snugger as he walked, it was worth it to build the sexual tension between them for a little longer.

Chapter Two

Where were they? She scanned the corrals as she made her way towards the cabin where she knew Kasey and Duncan lived. She had made a big dinner to thank them for how kind they had been to her since she arrived, and she wanted to catch them before they made other dinner plans.

Over the past few days, they'd put in such long hours. They seemed to work non-stop from dusk till dawn, so she had expected to find them in the barn cleaning up for the day like they normally were at this time. She glanced at her watch. It was Friday night, so maybe they'd packed it in a bit early so they could head into town.

She chewed on her lower lip. Shoot, she should have planned this on a different night. They were two gorgeous men. Of course, they'd have plans on a Friday night. She glanced at the cabin. The food was already in the oven, so it didn't hurt to see if they wanted to eat with her before they went out.

She knocked on the cabin door and heard what sounded like a grunt of acknowledgement. Men. She laughed. They couldn't just answer the door, no, they had to grunt from their place on the couch. Except when she pushed the door open, there was no one in the living room area. Weird.

From down the hall, she heard more noises, so she stepped further into the room.

"Yeah, that's it, take it deep," a male voice groaned. "Oh, fuck, Kase, you know I love when you do that with your tongue."

Julia stopped dead in tracks. Kasey and Duncan? Holy shit. She never would have expected that. They seemed so testosterone driven, a couple of alpha males. Clearly, she'd read all the flirtatious smiles and looks completely wrong. They had just been being nice to her, not hitting on her. God, she was a moron.

A deep male groan sounded from the other room.

"You like that, huh?" What sounded like Kasey's voice asked.

"You know I do. Now take it deep," Duncan ordered.

"Ah, fuck," he groaned.

Julia sucked in a breath. Oh my god, that was so hot. She needed to leave, but her feet felt glued to the floor. What kind of person listened to other people having sex? God, she was such a perv.

"Turn around and give me your ass," Duncan growled.

Her core muscles clenched as she listened to the sexual sounds coming from the bedroom. Her nipples beaded tightly, and she gripped the edge of the couch as her knees threatened to buckle. She bit back a groan of her own. God, listening to them was the most aroused she'd been in months.

"Jesus, you feel good," Duncan groaned.

She squeezed her thighs together, and her hand creeped towards the waistband of her jeans.

"No touching yourself, Kase. You'll come when I say you can," Duncan demanded.

God, what was wrong with her? She couldn't masturbate while she eavesdropped on them having sex. They were having sex in the privacy of their own home. She needed to get out of here.

She glanced towards the bedroom door one last time, then turned and fled the cabin.

Julia leaned against the side of the barn, breathing hard. She squeezed her legs together to try to curb the blood flowing to her core. She couldn't believe how turned on she was. Who knew listening to two men could be so freaking hot?

Guess she wasn't as cold as Tyler had said she was. Turns out maybe it was just him. Too bad what made her hot was the idea of being sandwiched between two sexy men. *Like that would ever happen.*

Julia shook her head. That kind of thing didn't happen. Sure, she had lots of sexy books in her collection that said otherwise, but it sure as shit didn't happen in real life to women like her. She pushed away from the barn. But at least she knew that part of her was still alive and well, despite all the evidence with Tyler to the contrary.

She walked back to the house and pushed open the door. The smell of lasagna and garlic hit her the moment she walked inside. What the hell was she going to do with all this food?

She chewed on her bottom lip. She could text them and ask them if they wanted dinner. Heat rose across her cheeks as she thought about seeing them after what she'd just heard. Could she handle sitting across the table from them?

Yes. She was a goddamn adult. Of course, she could sit across the table from two sexy men.

She'd come to Arizona to learn to stand up for herself, to get whole. She didn't need to be ashamed of who she was.

Being around Kasey and Duncan made her feel good. They made her feel beautiful and now that she knew they were a couple. It made all the flirting and looks they'd been giving her so nonthreatening. They were the perfect men to spend time with. Harmless. Safe. With them, she could practice getting comfortable around men again. Hopefully begin to believe she was beautiful and maybe, just maybe, become the person she had always dreamed of being. Someone strong and confident, someone who took no shit from anyone. Someone like Kat. Isn't that why she'd come here?

Decision made, she squared her shoulders and grabbed her phone. She created a group text with Kasey and Duncan.

Julia: I made lasagna if you don't have plans for dinner.

Duncan: We're in. When do you want us?

Now in my bed, Julia giggled to herself.

Julia: It'll be ready in about 20 minutes if that works for you.

Duncan: We'll be there. See you in a few.

Butterflies instantly danced in her stomach. She closed her eyes and breathed deeply in and out. She could do this. She was a grown up. Yes, she'd heard them having sex, but who cares. Nothing had changed.

She placed her hand against her stomach. Except everything had changed. Now she knew nothing would ever happen with them, not that it would have anyway, but she could relax. Sure, she might pull out her vibrator tonight as she remembered what she'd heard, but there was nothing wrong with that. She was human, after all, and they were two sexy-as- fuck men.

Julia opened the oven and pulled the tinfoil off the lasagna. The cheese bubbled across the top and she inhaled deeply. It looked perfect. She slid the loaf of garlic bread in down the side and closed the oven.

Hanging with Kasey and Duncan was exactly what she needed. She'd never really had male friends before. She'd always been a little uncomfortable with them. A little afraid of the power dynamic in male-female relationships after watching all her mom's failed relationships growing up. That was probably why she'd always dated meek men up until Tyler. Tyler was the first manly guy she'd dated and look at how that had turned out.

Intellectually, she knew not all manly men were abusive, like Tyler or the men her mom dated, but it was hard to tell that to her heart. She really hoped building a friendship with Kasey and Duncan would help her reconcile what she knew intellectually versus what life had taught her.

She pictured the two men and sighed. She'd never been around such powerful men before. Everything about them oozed testosterone, from the way they looked, the way their bodies moved with that male cocky swagger, to the jobs they did.

She'd watched them over the past couple of days, more than she should have, and against her better judgement, she'd felt incredibly drawn to them both. The easy way they were with each other, their kindness to the animals and to her. From what she'd seen, they were so different from the guys she knew. They seemed solid, safe, and Kat trusted them, which said a lot. She trusted Kat's judgment with men a lot more than her own.

Julia opened the cupboard door to grab the wine glasses. She leaned up on her tiptoes to reach for the glasses. A sound from behind her startled her, and she dropped the glass from her hand, causing it to shatter on the floor. Her heart raced. On instinct, she grabbed the olive oil bottle off the counter beside her as she turned around. When she saw Kasey and Duncan, she breathed a sigh of relief.

"Sorry, we probably should have knocked," Duncan said. His gaze scanned her body, then lingered on her hand with the bottle.

Embarrassed, she set the bottle on the counter. "You don't have to knock. I know you are all like one big family here. You just startled me, that's all."

"Don't move or you'll step in glass," Kasey told her. "I'm just going to grab the broom."

"You don't have to clean up. It's my mess," Julia told him. So much for proving she wasn't a basket case. The first sign of noise and she reacted like they were there to rob her. She looked down at her shaking hands and squeezed her fingers together.

Duncan crunched over the glass with his boots and stopped in front of her. "You okay?" he asked as he looked down at her clenched fists.

She shuddered out a breath. "I'm fine, it's nothing," she said as she forced her hands to open.

"Let's get you out of the way so Kasey can clean up the glass," Duncan said, as Kasey walked back in the room with the broom and dustpan.

"You okay if I touch you?" Duncan asked.

"Of course," she replied.

"Great," Duncan said, then grabbed hold of her hips and picked her and placed her bum on the edge of the counter. "Don't want you to cut your feet."

Duncan's hands lingered on her waist, and he didn't step back right away. Julia sucked in a breath at the look in his blue eyes as he held her stare. His fingers flexed against her hip. She licked her lips and his eyes followed the movement of her tongue.

"Alright, Romeo, you gonna move so I can sweep?" Kasey asked.

"Don't let me stand in the way of you cleaning," Duncan said. He glanced at Julia, winked, then stepped away from her. Whatever that moment had been was gone, making her wonder if it had even been there, or if it was just some weird leftover adrenaline surge.

She couldn't take her eyes off Kasey as he swept the floor. Never in a million years would she have expected a big, rugged man like Kasey to sweep the floor. She'd expected him to hand her the broom. The basic cleaning act looked like second nature as his muscular frame bent down to sweep the glass onto the dustpan. This man was nothing like her ex.

"So, what smells so good?" Duncan asked. He crouched down and peeked through the window in the oven. "Is that lasagna?"

Julia giggled and hopped down off the counter. She'd never seen anyone so excited about Italian food before. "It is. There's garlic bread and salad as well." The timer on the oven buzzed and Julia bumped Duncan with her hip to get him to shift over. She pulled open the oven and gave it a second before bending down to remove the food. "Would you mind pouring the wine? There's a bottle on the island," she asked Duncan.

"Not a problem." He leaned over the pan of lasagna and inhaled deeply. "Man, that smells fantastic." He rubbed his flat stomach. "This looks so much better than what we would have been eating tonight."

Julia smiled. "What was on the menu for you?"

Duncan shrugged. "Hadn't really thought about it too much. We probably would have headed into town and grabbed a burger or something."

"It's Friday night. You guys didn't have any big plans?"

"Nah, it was a long week with us being shorthanded," Kasey said when he walked back into the room after depositing the broom in the closet. Kasey stepped up beside her at the island and gazed at the pan of food in front of him. "Wow, Julia, this looks unreal. Thanks for asking us for dinner."

"No big deal. I miss cooking, and Kat has this amazing kitchen. I thought it would be fun to take advantage of it." She handed the breadbasket and salad bowl to Kasey. "Can you put that on the table for me?" she asked as she dished up large cheesy squares of lasagna onto plates. Kasey had taken a chair on one of the long sides of the table.

Duncan dropped his lean frame into the chair across from him on the other side of the table, leaving the head of the table for her. She eased into the chair, scanned the table to make sure she hadn't missed anything. When she looked up, both men were staring at her hungrily. "Sorry guys, dig in," she chuckled.

"Thank god," Kasey muttered.

"Wow," Duncan groaned around a mouthful of food.

Julia watched them dig into their first few bites. Other than the odd moan of appreciation, neither man spoke until they had devoured their entire plate of lasagna.

"Sheesh, you guys weren't kidding about having good appetites."

Kasey winced. "Sorry, normally we have a lot better manners than this. It was a long day and I'm not going to lie. I have never tasted anything like this in my life." He sopped up some tomato sauce on his plate with a piece of garlic bread. "Christ, Julia, when you said you were a cook, I think you kind of undersold yourself just a little."

"No kidding." Duncan laughed. "Kind of like saying Adele can carry a tune."

"Right?" Kasey snorted. "Just a little bit of an understatement.

Heat ran across Julia's cheeks as the men gushed over her cooking. She shifted uncomfortably in her chair. Hearing the compliments felt so foreign. It had been so long since someone had praised her.

She knew she was an excellent cook, but over the past few years with Tyler, her confidence about everything, including her skills in the kitchen, had taken a hit. How many meals had he pushed away or thrown out because they weren't up to his standards? Telling her she'd be lucky to get a job at a truck stop with the recipes she created.

She fiddled with the edge of the placemat. "Thanks," she murmured.

"No, thank you," Kasey gushed.

Duncan's hand touched the side of her wrist. "You okay?"

Julia's head whipped up. "What?"

"Sorry if we made you uncomfortable," he told her.

"No, no, you didn't." She smiled, shaking off her somber memories. "I'm glad you like it." She pushed up from the table and scooped up their plates. "Let me get you both some more."

"That would be awesome, thanks," Duncan told her.

As she cut more pieces of lasagna and added them to the plates, she could feel the men both watching her. What must they be thinking of her? What kind of person gets all flustered and weird from a compliment?

She squared her shoulders. No more. She was done with that shit. Tyler wasn't here, and she would not let his weaselly voice run on a loop in her brain anymore. The way the men had devoured their food, it was clear they didn't have the same opinion as Tyler, and that was more important.

She set the plates down in front of the men, determined to salvage the evening. "So how did you two meet?" she asked.

"We met on tour," Duncan told her as he ripped a piece of garlic bread in half.

"On tour? What kind of tour?" she asked.

"Rodeo?" Kasey replied.

"Like bulls and stuff?"

"Sort of... umm... we do different events than that," Duncan replied. "When we met, Kase was just doing steer wrestling, and I competed in tie-down and then we did team roping together once we became friends."

"Wow, so you guys are like legit cowboys. You ranch, you wrangle, you rope," she teased.

"Well now, darlin'," Kasey drawled. "There's more to being a cowboy than just wrangling and roping."

"Oh, yeah?" She rested her chin on her hand and leaned towards him. "What else is there?"

Kasey's gaze ran across her face, then down her neck, to her breasts, then slowly back up to her eyes. She felt his stare like a caress. Everywhere his eyes lingered, her body responded. Her nipples pulled tight against her shirt.

"You gotta know how to take your time and go slow to tame a wild horse," he said, his voice sounded gritty and tight as he spoke.

She sucked in a breath at the heat in his hazel eyes as he held her stare.

"How do you know when the horse is ready for more?" she whispered.

"If you're patient, it comes to you," he told her.

"It does," she murmured.

Kasey stood up and leaned over her. He brushed the hair from her cheek and tucked it behind her ear. "It's not always easy to be patient, but when you are, it's always worth the wait," he whispered, then started clearing the dishes from the table.

She looked over at Duncan, who was watching them with a look of pure male interest on his face. Wowza, the man was potent. Julia swallowed past the dryness in her throat. God, was it hot in here?

What was happening? They were gay. Weren't they?

Duncan's gaze roamed down her body, then back to her face. She was mesmerized by his mouth as his tongue darted out through his beard and swiped along his lip before he pulled his bottom lip between his teeth and held it. His nostrils flared as he held her stare. "Definitely worth the wait." He stood and grabbed his plate off the table.

And holy shit, why the hell were they so good at flirting?

Julia looked at the two men loading the dishwasher like they didn't have a care in the world. Maybe she'd just imagined the sexual innuendo in that conversation. She squeezed her legs together. Her body sure as sugar thought he was suggesting something might happen between them. But maybe that was just wishful thinking on her part. She chewed her bottom lip as she watched them.

Her plans for having safe fantasies about her gay friends would go right out the window if they liked women.

Duncan swaggered towards the table. "Don't overthink it, darlin'. You just got here. Relax. Get your bearings. We'll have you riding in no time." He tapped the tip of her nose with his finger, then headed back to the kitchen island with his dishes.

Now she was more confused than ever. What the hell did that mean? *We'll get you riding in no time*, she grumbled. That didn't even make sense. *We'll get you riding.*

Like there was a 'we' with all of them together. Gah, men. They were so confusing. *So much for having them figured out.*

She eyed her empty wineglass. Shit, that stuff was potent, because her mind was definitely not working right tonight. Hearing the men having sex together earlier, followed by a nice evening and wine, had clearly scrambled her brain. No more wine for her.

Julia pressed her palms against the table and pushed herself up.

"Who needs coffee?" she asked.

*****

How was it possible she had already been on the ranch for ten days? In some ways, she felt like her arrival had been a lifetime ago and in others; it felt like she had just gotten here.

Julia curled up in the corner of the couch with a plush cushion behind her back. She closed her eyes and listened to the sounds in the kitchen. Kat and Justin had gotten home from their honeymoon this afternoon. Shortly after they'd arrived, Kat had sent Justin out with his friends to give them some time to catch up.

Now Julia was just waiting for the inquisition to begin. She rolled her neck back and forth along the back of the sofa to ease the tension at the base of her skull.

"You mind if I steal this blanket?" she asked, indicating the blanket draped over the arm of the leather recliner.

"Nope, it's all yours," Kat replied as she came back into the room carrying two glasses of red wine. She handed Julia a glass, then sat down on the other end of the couch and pulled her knees up on the sofa.

"So, Jules, why are you really here?"

She'd known this conversation was coming. How could it not be? But that didn't make it any easier. Kat was so strong and kick-ass, she wouldn't understand the situation Julia had allowed herself to get into. "I told you, I just missed you."

"Right." Kat stared until Julia started to squirm. Crap, Kat had always been good at getting the bottom of things. It was what made her such a talented reporter. But as a friend, sometimes it sucked.

Julia sighed. *Well, here goes nothing.* "I did miss you. That part wasn't a lie. The other, Kat, I don't know. I just am kind of embarrassed to admit to you."

"Why? What could possibly be that bad?"

She set her drink down and scrubbed her hands over her face. "It's complicated."

Kat slid across the sofa and set her hand on Julia's knee. "Sweetie, come on, we've been friends forever. There's nothing you can't tell me."

"Right." She took a deep breath and exhaled. Here goes nothing. "Basically, I'm a complete idiot and I didn't know where else to go."

"What do you mean? What happened?"

"As you know, I'd been dating this guy Tyler for the past few years."

"Right." Kat shifted forward in her chair, so she was fully facing Julia. The simple shift in posture made Julia smile. It was such a Kat move. She was about drawing people in when they talked. Julia had always envied Kat and how good she was at making people feel comfortable, so they felt safe. Hell, it was why she'd come here, because she knew Kat wouldn't judge her. She was probably the only person she knew who wouldn't, but that didn't make it any easier to open up and talk about what happened.

Kat touched Julia's knee. "Talk to me, sweetie. Whatever it is, we'll figure it out."

Julia squeezed Kat's hand back. "Thanks. It's just ... God, look at you, Kat. You are so strong. You have your shit together and look at me. I show up on your doorstep after not talking to you for the past two years. I'm broke and...." She bit back the tears that threatened to fall. How had she allowed herself to get into this situation?

"Maybe let's start with what happened with Tyler. I'm assuming you two broke up?" Kat asked.

"Sort of, not really. I mean, I left, so I guess we broke up." She sighed. "I kind of just packed my bags and fled while he was at work. "

Kat's back straightened. "Fled?"

Shit. Julia squirmed. Kat's reporter nose had caught a scent. "Why did you need to flee?"

Julia shrugged. "I guess I'd just finally had enough. I mean... I had nothing. He was angry all the time." She chewed her bottom lip as she thought about what things had been like living there. "I don't know how I allowed myself to become this person."

"Who do you think you've become?" Kat asked quietly.

"Someone pathetic... like my mother." Tears welled in her eyes. "How did I become a person who let a guy make her feel like this? God, I always thought my mom was so weak dating all these guys who treated her like shit, using her as a punching bag and a meal ticket, and I'm not any better." Julia dropped her face into her hands.

"So, Tyler hit you?" Kat asked.

"Just once." She raised her head and met Kat's stare. "That's why I finally left," she whispered. Jesus, it was so hard to admit that out loud.

"Okay, so that's good that you left." Kat dropped on to her knees in front of Julia and pulled her in to a hug. "You aren't like your mom, sweetie. You left. She never could do that."

"That's true, I guess." She rested her head on Kat's shoulder. "But I allowed all the other stuff. I worked my ass off the entire time we were together and what do I have to show for it? Nothing. I was a fucking idiot who had my paychecks direct deposited into an account I can't access. I had to beg for money to put gas in my own car and it was my money. Who does that?"

"Oh honey," Kat murmured. "How long into the relationship did he start putting you down?"

Julia shrugged. "I don't know. It's not like it was all bad. I mean, he could be really sweet. When we first started dating, he made me feel so special. Like I was the most beautiful woman in the room." She smiled sadly as she thought back on what that had been like. "I'd never had that before. I've never really felt like anyone's first choice, you know?" She pushed back from Kat. "I'm okay, you can sit back down," she told Kat.

Kat slid back into her seat. "So, I'm guessing you guys moved in together?"

"Yeah, and things were great for the first little bit. Then I guess he just saw what everyone else has always seen in me and things changed."

"What do you mean, 'what everyone else always did'?" Kat asked.

"I don't know. You know how klutzy I can be, and how I don't always think before I speak."

Kat's eyes narrowed. "And let me guess he had something to say about that?"

Julia shrugged. "Well, yeah, I mean, it can be embarrassing when I put my foot in my mouth." She thought back to the beginning of her relationship. "I'm not great with money, as you know, and Tyler really was. So it made sense to let him take care of paying the bills and stuff so that I didn't get to the end of the month with more month than money. It was helpful at first, but then..." She sighed. "Then it got to feel a bit much, you know?"

Kat nodded.

"Little by little, it just got harder and harder. I look in the mirror and I don't even recognize myself. Tyler didn't like when I put on any extra weight, so I watched everything I put in my mouth, but god I was hungry all the time, and I don't like the way I look like this." She gestured to her body.

Julia looked over at Kat and could tell her friend had something she wanted to say. "Spit it out, Kat. It's not like you to hold your tongue."

Kat opened her mouth to speak, closed it, and sighed. The compassion on her face nearly brought tears to Julia's eyes again. Crap, this wasn't going to be good.

Kat slid forward and met Julia's stare. "Sweetie, just because he didn't hit you before doesn't mean he wasn't abusive."

"No, no, I just probably wasn't explaining it very well. It's nothing like my mom's relationships. And as soon as he hit me, I got the hell out of there," Julia argued.

"I know and I really proud of you. It can't have been easy." Kat smiled sadly. "But Jules, there are all kinds of abuse, and you know that. It wasn't just the hitting you hated about your mom's boyfriends. It was how shitty they made her feel about herself, how worthless they made her feel. How she questioned every decision she made." Kat paused. "From what you told me, that sounds like what Tyler did with you. It started out great, but then he made you feel like shit about everything about yourself until you believed him."

Tears burned in the back of her eyes. *Shit.* "I left when he hit me," she whispered. Shame knotted in her gut. How could she have been so weak? She needed to hold on to the fact that she'd been strong enough to leave when it escalated to violence, otherwise—Shit, it didn't bear thinking about.

Kat wiped away the tears streaming down her own cheeks. "I know you did, honey, and I'm so glad you came here."

Julia sniffed and wiped her face with her sleeve. "How did I become my fucking mother?"

"You made a different choice," Kat told her. "You're here now and we are going to figure this out." Kat took a sip of her wine and set the glass down. "You can stay here as long as you want," she said.

"I can't do that to you, Kat. You are newlyweds. The last thing you want is someone else living with you and cramping your style. I'll stay for a few more days, then I'll figure something out."

"Honestly, there's no rush. Justin doesn't mind you being here at all. And don't worry about the newlywed thing. He's very creative about getting what he wants, so you won't be cramping anything. He'll enjoy the challenge."

Julia laughed. "God, now I really need to get out of your hair because lord knows what I'll walk in on."

Kat blushed.

"Oh, my god. Spill," Julia demanded.

"We might have gotten caught having sex in the pool at the resort on our honeymoon."

Julia coughed. "What? Why... Wh... who are you, and what have you done with my straightlaced friend?"

Kat giggled. "Like I said, he can be very persuasive."

"Clearly." Julia laughed. "I'm really happy for you, Kat. You deserve it."

"Thanks." Kat squeezed her hand. "So do you. And despite all the shit that your asshole ex told you, I'm going to make it my mission to help you believe it. There's no better place to heal and figure out what you want out of life than this ranch. It certainly gave me a lot of clarity when I came here, and I know it can do the same for you."

Julia laughed. "Yeah, well, I think a sexy cowboy might have helped a lot."

Kat waggled her eyebrows. "Well, there are certainly more than enough of those to go around. You have seen the guys around here, haven't you?"

"Oh, I've definitely seen them. Do they allow unattractive men to live here?"

Kat grinned. "Nope, they stop them at the county line."

"Well, at least I have lots of eye candy to look at. I'm not sure I'm ready for anything else." She thought about all the things Tyler had said about how useless and ugly she was. "Or that they'd even want me," she murmured.

Kat's eyes narrowed. "Any man would want you, Julia. That's just your asshole ex talking."

Shit, she hadn't meant to say that out loud. She looked down at her hands and nodded.

"Plus, your asshole ex wanted you, whether or not he let you believe it, or else he would have moved on as well. If you were so awful, wouldn't he have left?" Kat asked.

"I never really thought about it like that," Julia reeled as the reality of what Kat said hit her. Was Kat right?

"Well, start. You are a beautiful woman, Jules. You always have been. Guys have always noticed you. You just rarely noticed them looking at you for whatever reason." Kat looked at her and held her stare. "You are one of the kindest people I know. You always see the best in people and give them the benefit of the doubt. You are a catch. It's more likely Tyler knew you were out of his league and berated you, so you didn't realize it and move on to better things."

Holy shit, Kat was right. If she was so useless, Tyler would have left, but he didn't. He came home every night. He never cheated on her. He tried to control everyone she came in contact with. That had to mean something.

"Thanks, Kat."

"Anytime, sweetie. You know I've got your back."

"I know you do, and I really appreciate it." Julia smiled at her best friend. This was why she had come to Kat. She knew she had made the right decision tracking her down. Now she just had to figure out what to do with the rest of her life because she couldn't rely on the kindness of Kat and her new husband forever.

"Do you have a job you need to get back to?" Kat asked.

Shame knotted her stomach, and she looked down at the wineglass in her hands, unable to meet Kat's eyes. "No, I, umm... I quit about a month ago." She trailed her finger around the rim of her glass. "Tyler didn't like me working at night when he was home, so..." She shrugged.

"So, he made you quit your job?" Kat growled.

"Yeah, it made sense at the time," Julia said. "Now, obviously, it seems pretty stupid."

"It seems like it put you in a pretty vulnerable situation. I imagine you felt even more stuck once you gave up your ability to earn money. You didn't even have the option of getting a new bank account to funnel your paycheck into," Kat said kindly.

Julia wiped the tear that escaped from the corner of her eye. "Like I said, pretty stupid."

Kat squeezed her hand. "You're here now and we'll get you back on your feet in no time."

"I hope so," Julia whispered.

"Trust me," Kat told her, "You got this."

The sound of the front door opening followed by loud, boisterous male voices put a halt to their conversation.

Justin stopped in his tracks. "Shit, did we interrupt something?"

Kat glanced at Julia, then back at her husband. "No, we were done. You're fine. Come on in."

"Did you guys have fun at the game?" Julia asked.

"Yeah, the Wildcats kicked some ass," Kasey said as he dropped onto the end of the couch where Julia was sitting.

Kasey smiled at her. "You okay?"

"Yeah, I'm good, thanks."

He continued to study her. When he looked at her like that, he seemed to see everything she wasn't saying. No one had ever looked at her with the intensity that Kasey did. Like he actually wanted to know what was going on in her brain.

Duncan dropped onto the couch between them, breaking their connection. "So, what did you ladies get up to?" He looked between Kat and Julia. "Talk about sex? Maybe have a pillow fight?" He waggled his eyebrows.

Kat laughed. "Yeah, you caught us. We had a pillow fight in our underwear."

Duncan grabbed his chest. "Damn, I knew I should have skipped the game. Did you videotape it?"

A couch pillow flew across the room and hit Duncan squarely in the face. He picked up the pillow and laughed as he chucked it back at Justin, who stood scowling at him.

"Stop flirting with my wife, you ass," Justin growled.

"Ah, you're just jealous because she finds me more charming than you," Duncan joked.

He turned to Julia and smiled. "Seriously, you okay? Were you guys able to get some time to talk about everything?"

"Yeah, we did, thanks." She squeezed his hand in appreciation for his kindness.

These men were amazing. So different from all the guys she'd spent time with growing up. Kat was really lucky to have these kinds of men in her life. Men who honestly cared what a woman said and didn't treat her like she didn't have a brain in her head or that she was disposable.

Kasey and Duncan were so different from each other, but from what she'd learned about them over the past several days, at the core, they were both just really nice men. Kasey had a quiet intensity that was incredibly sexy. The way he watched a person, like he wanted to truly understand them, and cared enough to listen when they talked. She didn't know guys like that actually existed.

And Duncan, well shit. Duncan was just sex personified. Everything about the man oozed sex appeal and confidence. He was always joking and flirting to lighten the mood, but he honestly seemed to give people the benefit of the doubt and treat people really kindly. Of course, they were gay. Mystical unicorns like these two guys just didn't exist in the real world.

Julia looked around the room. Justin had slid into the chair with Kat and pulled her up on his lap, so they snuggled in the large recliner. Kat looked so incredibly happy, and it brought a smile to Julia's face. If anyone deserved that kind of love, it was Kat.

The men bantered back and forth while she sat soaking in the feelings of friendship and love in the room. She hadn't felt this safe and happy in years. She couldn't imagine leaving.

"Do any of you happen to know anyone who is hiring around here?" Julia asked.

"You planning on sticking around?" Duncan asked.

She shrugged. "I'd really like to if I can find a job." She looked over at Justin. "Don't worry, I don't plan on staying with you guys. I just would like to stay in the area now that I've found Kat again and..." she trailed off. It was embarrassing to admit she had nowhere else to go. Over the past two years with Tyler, she'd drifted apart from all of her friends and supports, and she'd stopped talking to her mother when she left home at 16. Besides Kat, she couldn't think of a single person who cared about her.

She hadn't realized how lonely she was until she'd come to this ranch. The week she'd spent with Kasey and Duncan had made her feel connected, and like she was a part of something. Now reconnecting with Kat, she felt like she could really have a home here.

"What kind of work are you looking for?" Justin asked.

"Honestly, I'd do pretty much anything." She was ashamed to admit just how little money she had to her name. She'd been desperate when she'd arrived here, but she couldn't rely on the kindness of Kat and her new husband forever.

"I told you that you can stay with us as long as you want to," Kat said.

"I know, and I really appreciate that, but I can't keep sponging off you. I need to get a job and at least some room and board until I can afford to get set up on my own."

"She's a hell of a cook," Duncan said.

"You always loved to bake and stuff when we were growing up." Kat smiled. "I remember those dump cookies you used to make where you would just grab whatever you could find and throw it all together. My god, those were always amazing even when they shouldn't have been."

Julia groaned. "They weren't always good. I'm not sure what I was thinking putting peppermint and peanut butter together."

Kat laughed. "It was Christmas. They needed candy cane pieces and come on; everything goes with peanut butter."

Julia pictured the monster cookies with M&M's, candy cane pieces, and pretzels.

"She's not wrong," Kasey agreed. "They sound pretty good to me."

Julia looked over to find Justin watching her intently. She dropped her head down and looked at her hands.

"Would you be open to cooking and cleaning work?" Justin asked.

"She's been cooking for us since she's been here, and I can tell you she's freaking amazing." Kasey stood and walked towards the kitchen. "Dunc and I have never eaten so well in our lives." He lifted his shirt and looked at his stomach. "It's a good thing we do physical work, otherwise things could go sideways in a hurry."

Julia's eyes lingered on the trail of hair that ran from his belly button down tight washboard abs and disappeared into his jeans. She bit her bottom lip. Duncan nudged her with his thigh, and she ripped her stare off Kasey's stomach. "You're drooling a little," Duncan whispered.

Heat raced across her face. "Oh my god," she murmured.

Duncan chuckled beside her. "Don't worry about it. All the ladies have that reaction to Kase with his shirt off."

Kasey pulled his shirt back down. "Shut up."

"What? You know it's true," Duncan teased.

"He's not lying," Kat joined in and laughed when Justin growled.

"So back to my question, would you want a job cooking and cleaning?" Justin asked.

"Yeah, I'd love that. Before I stopped working, I was an executive chef back in California," Julia shared.

"Wow." Justin rubbed the back of his neck. "Umm, then I probably wouldn't keep you for very long, but uh, at least until you find something closer to what you deserve. We've been talking about hiring someone to cook and clean between here and my sister's place."

"Oh my god, yes, she'd be perfect," Kat agreed. "I don't know why I didn't think of that."

"I mean, I know it's not restaurant chef gig or anything even close to that, but we could do room and board plus like $1500 a month or something. I know it's not at all what you are used to, and you have no obligation to say yes," Justin continued.

"Yes," Julia yelled. "Absolutely yes."

Justin laughed. "Alright then. Looks like you have yourself a job."

Kat smacked a loud kiss on Justin's lips, then turned to Julia. "This is going to be amazing."

"Welcome aboard," Duncan said. Julia turned to him, and he held out his arms for a hug. She leaned into him, allowing his warmth to wrap around her. His warm breath hit the side of her neck and goosebumps broke out across her neck. She looked up and made eye contact with Kasey. The heat in his stare had her sucking in a breath. Wow, what was that about?

Duncan let her go and glanced at Kasey, then back at Julia, and grinned. "Oh yeah, Kat's right. This is going to be awesome."

"This is my best friend, you guys. Make good choices," Kat said, looking back and forth between Kasey and Duncan.

The men looked at each other, and with matching expressions of innocence, they raised their hands. "Don't we always," Kasey asked.

Duncan turned to Julia and winked. "Plus, it always feels so good to be bad."

Julia glanced at Kasey, who smiled at her like he was picturing her naked. Julia's nipples beaded tightly beneath his heated stare.

Holy crap, what was happening? Man, they were potent. It's a good thing they were gay, or she'd never be able to resist them, and how would a girl choose between these two men?

Julia fanned her face. "Alright, you two, knock it off." Julia laughed and pushed Duncan away from her.

Kat gave her a puzzled look that Julia didn't really understand. Needing to get her body back under control, Julia turned her attention back to Justin. "When could I start?"

"As soon as you want," Justin replied. "Dee and I were talking about having someone clean her place once a week, our place once a week and then the staff cabins might need cleaned monthly, just to make sure they don't get too bad. I don't want to ask you to go in there more than once a month because lord knows what you might see."

Julia thought back to what she had heard the last time she had gone into Duncan and Kasey's place, and heat bloomed across her cheeks.

"What's the look for?" Kat asked.

Duncan nudged her with his shoulder. "I think our girl here might be a bit of a voyeur."

"What? No, I'm not," she argued, but when she met Duncan's knowing smirk, she blushed even harder.

"Whatever you say." Duncan laughed.

Kasey smacked Duncan on the back of the head. "Leave her alone. Stop embarrassing her, you ass."

"Sorry Jules, I was just teasing you," Duncan replied.

"I know. It's totally fine." She smiled back at him.

"What about meals? What were you thinking there?" Julia asked Justin.

"I'll let you talk to Dee yourself to be sure, but when we talked, she was thinking of having someone cook up some meals that her and Brody could heat up during the week and that would be enough. We normally do a big Sunday dinner with everyone here. We typically all fend for ourselves for breakfast and then the guys and I do lunch together and whoever is around joins us for dinner. How does that sound?"

"It sounds amazing," Julia replied. The idea of cooking for people again, doing what she loved, felt unreal. Being accepted into this amazing household with Kat and her new family was a gift she hadn't expected when she'd fled to Arizona. For the first time in longer than she could remember, she felt safe and accepted.

She made eye contact with Kat and mouthed. "Thank you."

Kat smiled and winked back at her.

"So, when can we talk about the menu?" she asked Justin. "Is there anything you don't like to eat? Do you like to eat the same things each week or is variety okay? I could maybe do like themed weeks or something," she rambled excitedly.

"Looks like you've unleashed the beast with this job, Jus," Duncan joked.

"Sorry," Julia murmured. "I got a little excited."

"No, don't apologize. I love it," Justin told her. "Normally, cooking around here is a chore that no one wants to do. We've hired a couple of house mangers that didn't work out, so it's been a bit of a gong show for the past few months around here. If your food is as good as what the guys say, then I can't wait to have you cook for us."

"If I can borrow a car, I can hit the grocery store tomorrow, if that's okay," Julia told him.

"Kasey and Duncan were heading into town tomorrow to pick up some supplies, so you could all go in together tomorrow morning," Justin said. "You guys good with that?"

"Works for us," Kasey replied.

Julia smiled at Kasey. "Great."

She turned to Justin. "Thanks again. I won't let you down."

"I know you won't," Justin said with a smile.

Julia fought the urge to get up and do a little happy dance. Things were looking up.

Chapter Three

Julia giggled as she walked towards the foreman's cabin. She really needed to find a place of her own and give Justin and Kat their space. Her eyes were still burning from walking in on them today in the kitchen. She was going to have to sanitize that counter now that she'd seen her best friend spread out naked on top of it while her sexy husband ate her for an afternoon snack.

It never occurred to her she might walk in on that in the middle of the workday. The men never took breaks. Guess that was the perk of being the boss and a newlywed. From now on, she'd make sure she sang when she was coming back into the house.

She pushed open the door to the cabin and looked around. The men were remarkably tidy. It wouldn't take long at all to clean their place once a month. She placed the dishes in the sink and filled up the kitchen sink with hot soapy water. Leaving the dishes to soak for a couple minutes, she wandered down the hall to the bathroom to add cleaner to the toilet to let it sit for a bit. She reached under the bathroom sink and heard grunting from the bedroom.

Oh shit. Not again. Crap, why did she keep coming in here when they were having sex?

She turned to leave the bathroom and banged her hip against the open cupboard door. The impact nearly knocked the cabinet door off its hinge. "Fuck," she groaned in pain.

The bedroom door flew open, and a shirtless Kasey stared at her wide eyed. "Uh hey, Jules."

"Hi, sorry I didn't know you were home, otherwise I would have knocked." She stared at his broad, muscular, naked chest. She could feel her cheeks burning and knew her face would be bright red. Awesome.

Duncan walked out of the bedroom in jeans and t-shirt. His sun-streaked hair standing up in every direction, the only indication that something had been going on. He smirked when he looked between her and Kasey.

Julia rubbed her thigh where she'd bashed it and tried not to make eye contact with the men.

"We were just moving some furniture," Kasey said.

Duncan snorted. "Yep, we moved some furniture all right."

Kasey's head whipped towards Duncan, who raised his eyebrows mockingly. Julia bit back a smile of her own. "Sure," she murmured. "I can come back later if you want?" she asked.

"Nah, you're here now and we've, umm, already finished moving the furniture." Duncan smirked.

Kasey growled and pushed past Duncan out of the hallway towards the kitchen. "Do you want coffee or anything?" Kasey called over his shoulder.

She looked at Duncan, who was observing her.

She needed to come clean to the guys and admit this wasn't the first time she'd heard them and that they didn't have to sneak around. Time to pay the piper. "Sure, I'd love some," she said, making her way down the hall.

"What do you take in your coffee?" Kasey asked.

"Milk and sugar, but I can doctor it up myself," she replied.

"Nah, you go sit. I've got it," Kasey said.

She glanced at Duncan, who was sitting in the Lazyboy beside the fireplace, and she plopped down on the loveseat across from him. Kasey handed her the mug and sat down beside her.

She took a fortifying sip of the coffee and immediately wished it had some whiskey or something in it when she still didn't feel prepared to have this conversation.

"So, umm, about the furniture moving." Julia glanced at Duncan, then Kasey.

Duncan smirked. "Uh huh, what about it?"

"This is really awkward. You don't have to pretend you were moving furniture. I'm fully aware of what was actually going on."

"Oh yeah, what was going on in there, Jules?" Duncan asked, grinning.

"Don't be an asshole," Kasey growled.

"How am I being an asshole?" Duncan asked. "We're all adults here. Plus, Jules is cute when she's blushing."

Julia rolled her eyes. "No woman over the age of 12 likes to be called cute."

"What would you like me to call you? Most of the time you're just sexy, but the blush is different. It's kind of sweet and changes the mood a little, so cute, felt like it worked."

Warmth spread through her body at Duncan, calling her sexy. She met his stare and was surprised at the heat in his blue eyes. *Get a grip*, she told herself. She had literally just heard him having sex with Kasey. Any heat she was seeing was left over from that. Not directed at her.

"Right, anyway," she continued. "I know you guys were having sex. I'm not an idiot. Plus, umm... well... it's not the first time I've heard you guys."

"What?" Kasey yelped. "When else have you heard us?"

Heat burned her cheeks. "Umm...when I first got here, I came over to talk to you and heard you."

Duncan laughed. "Kase is a moaner."

Kasey glared at Duncan and Julia burst out laughing. "Actually, it was you I heard," she said to Duncan.

Duncan smiled and shrugged. "Busted."

He leaned back in his chair and crossed his ankle over his knee, and looked at her. "You know, anytime you want to join in, you just have to say." He waggled his eyebrows. "The more the merrier."

Oh my. Even the thought of that had moisture pooling in her core. "Ha-ha, very funny."

"Maybe you prefer to just watch," Duncan continued.

Julia cleared her throat. "Anyway. I just wanted you to know that you don't have to hide your relationship with me. We're friends. I want you to just be yourself around me."

"I appreciate that," Kasey said and squeezed her hand.

"Well, that went better than I'd hoped and a lot less awkward than what I walked in on with Kat and Justin before I came over here today." *Lord, that was embarrassing.*

"You got an eyeful, did you?" Duncan grinned.

"Oh, my god. Let's just say that kitchen is getting well sanitized before I cook anything."

Kasey laughed. "Justin always did have a healthy appetite."

Julia looked over and rolled her eyes. "I really need to find a new place to live. Those two go at it like rabbits and who can blame them? I mean, they're newlyweds, for god's sakes. They should be able to have sex wherever and whenever the mood strikes in their own house, and I feel like I'm seriously cramping their style."

"We've got an extra room if you want to move in here," Duncan told her.

"I don't want to cramp your style either," Julia told him.

"Yeah, but the difference is we don't mind if you watch, or join in."

Zowie. Her nipples beaded tightly beneath her bra. "I'll keep that in mind," she laughed. "Are you sure you guys wouldn't mind if I moved into your spare room? I   just

—." She shrugged. "Kat and Justin have been so kind to me, allowing me to stay here, giving me a job. I just don't want them to resent me being here."

"The room is empty. You're more than welcome to use it. We'd love to have you stay here with us. And Duncan was just being an idiot on the sex in public thing. We can be discreet, so you aren't uncomfortable."

"It doesn't make me uncomfortable at all," Julia told him. Well, not the kind of uncomfortable he was talking about.

Kasey continued to look at her, assessing her. His eyes scanned down her body, lingering on her nipples, where she was sure they were sticking straight out of her shirt like a beacon. His nostrils flared. "You can move in whenever you want. We'll give you all the space you want or don't want."

Julia glanced at Duncan, who was also staring at her breasts. What the hell was going on here? She was so confused. She shuddered out a breath.

Julia pushed off the couch and set her coffee mug in the kitchen sink. "I've got to get back to work. But I'll maybe move in this weekend if that works for you guys."

Duncan cleared his throat. "That more than works for us."

She could feel both men watching her as she left the cabin. What had she just agreed to?

*****

Friday afternoon Julia looked up from hanging the clothes on the line to see Kat's truck pull up. Holy cow, how could it be that late already? She flicked a glance at her watch. Two o'clock. Okay, not late at all. What the heck was Kat doing home already?

"Hey, you almost done there?" Kat yelled across the yard.

"Yeah, just about. Why?"

"I'm playing hooky this afternoon, so's Dee and we're taking you out for a girl's night."

"At two o'clock in the afternoon?"

Kat shrugged. "Things are different here in Arizona." She laughed. "Nah, I'm just kidding. It's ladies' night at this club downtown, and what can I say? There will be dancers involved."

"Dancers? As in strippers."

Kat's eyes twinkled with amusement. "Don't sound so scandalized. I've seen you at the strippers before."

"I know, but that was a lo-ong time ago. Things have changed since then. I've changed."

"That's kind of the point, sweetie." Kat smiled sadly. "You used to be this wild, carefree girl and now you're just... I don't know." She wrapped her arm around Julia's shoulder. "I miss that girl, and I know she's in there."

Julia rested her head on Kat's shoulder. She missed that girl, too. "Okay, let's see if we can find her. But later. I still have work to finish," she said, bending to pick up the laundry basket.

Kat grabbed it out of her hand. "Oh, no you don't. Dee and I already decided we're in the mood for some shopping first."

"Can't you do that part without me?" Julia groaned. "Ouch." She rubbed the top of her head where Kat's knuckles had landed. "I can't believe you did that."

"Oh, come on. You can't say something ridiculous like that and not get cracked."

Julia couldn't help but laugh. Her dad used to say the same thing to them all the time when they were little. He used to rap them on the head a lot harder too to get the point across. Guess she should be thankful for small favors. "Fine. What are we shopping for?"

"Oh my god, Julia." Kat rolled her eyes. "Where did I go wrong with you? All that training in high school and it was all for nothing." She placed her hands on her hips and looked Julia up and down. "I've got my work cut out for me."

Julia looked down at her baggy jeans and t-shirt. They'd fit fine six months ago before her life had turned to shit, and she'd been too depressed to eat. Okay, maybe Kat was right, and she needed a little help.

"Alright, Sensei, lead the way," Julia said sarcastically.

"Sensei, I like that." Kat's head bobbed up and down. "Yep, I definitely like it." Kat hitched the laundry basket up on one hip and slung her other arm around Julia's shoulder. "Now, young grasshopper, in order to get you back on the horse, we must first get you not smelling like you bathed in cleaning supplies." She grimaced. "Not sexy."

"Fine, shower first, then shopping," Julia said through gritted teeth. Shopping. God. She'd rather stick toothpicks in her eyes. There better be drinks involved, because that was the only way she was going to get through this.

Kat bumped her hip against Julia's and grinned. "Don't worry, Dee's already got the blender going for margaritas. You can drink it while you get ready."

"You know me so well," Julia said with a smile.

Kat's arm squeezed around her neck, pulling her closer. "Yeah, I do, which is how I know you need this. So, trust me, okay?"

"There's no one I trust more. That's why I'm here, right?" Julia looked at her oldest friend. They'd been through so much together growing up. The death of Julia's dad, her mom's string of bad relationships, Kat's parents' complete lack of interest in anything Kat did, and everything in between. Together, they'd made it through everything. She'd get through this too.

"Alright, bring on the booze."

Kat whooped. "That's more like it."

Several hours later, the three women made their way through the club to find seats to watch the show. Julia had to admit, as much as she hated the whole shopping experience, she felt incredible in her new clothes. Even if it had been humbling to have to let her best friend buy them for her. Kat had insisted she wear them out of the store.

When their drinks were set down in front of them, Julia eyed the waiter's bare, muscular chest. Mmm, there was something to be said for the atmosphere, that's for sure.

"Not bad, huh?" Kat asked with a grin.

"Not bad at all." Maybe Kat was right, and she needed to get back in the game. Tyler had been a mistake. One she'd definitely learned from. Maybe what she needed was just some fun. To let loose a little. Unfortunately, she couldn't get the image of Kasey and Duncan out of her mind. Too bad they were gay because ever since she'd heard them together, she hadn't been able to think of anything else.

Curiosity getting the best of her, she asked, "So tell me about Kasey and Duncan."

Kat smirked. "What do you want to know?"

"Umm." Everything. "How long have they been a couple?"

Denise sputtered, and her drink spewed across the table. She coughed to clear her throat. Her eyes danced with laughter as she looked at Julia. "Kasey and Duncan aren't a couple."

"What the hell would you call them?" She didn't know too many guys who fucked each other as often as they did that weren't a couple.

"Uh friends," Denise replied.

"Some friends," she murmured.

"What are you talking about?" Denise asked.

Julia looked over at Kat, who was trying very hard to look anywhere but at her. What was that about? Oh crap, maybe they didn't want everyone to know about them.

Great. "My mistake, I guess, I must have misread them because they're such close friends or something." Shit, she hadn't meant to out them. When Kasey had said Justin and Kat knew, she thought that meant Denise knew as well.

Denise took a sip of her drink, then nodded. "Yeah, that must be it because they are definitely into women, aren't they, Kat?" Denise blinked innocently at the other woman.

"Uh." Kat stared at the table.

"Oh my god, you slept with one of them?"

"Uh... well..." Kat stammered.

Denise snorted. Kat's head snapped up, and she scowled.

"What?" Julia looked back and forth between the two women. "What am I missing?"

"Umm... well." Kat played with the coaster on the table.

"Umm, well, what?" Julia demanded.

Kat raised her head and chewed her bottom lip. "I might have had a little, um, weekend thing with them."

Julia's eyes boggled open. "Holy shit, you slept with Kasey and Duncan? What about Justin? Was this before you hooked up?"

Kat blushed. "Umm. No, Justin was there."

Denise snickered and picked up her drink. "Just spill it. You were all braggy to me about it, and it was my brother, so no need to be embarrassed now."

Kat scowled at Denise. "That was different. Justin and I were figuring everything out."

"I'll say," Denise murmured.

"Spill," Julia ordered.

Kat straightened her shoulders. "Fine. Umm, well, when I first came here, Justin and I immediately hit it off and things were intense, to say the least." Kat paused and took a sip of her drink.

"Uh huh," Julia prodded.

"And we maybe had a dirty weekend with his friends."

"Like a gang bang?" Julia screeched.

"It wasn't a gang bang," Kat muttered.

Denise choked on her drink, causing it to come out of her nose.

"Okay, maybe it was." Kat laughed. "God, it sounds so filthy when you say it like that."

"It was filthy." Denise snickered. "But take my brother out of the equation and it sounded hotter than hell, too."

"Oh my," Julia said. She thought of the passionate groans she had heard between the two men. She'd already been fantasizing about being with them, but that had been fantasy when she thought they were gay. Knowing they were also into women put a whole new spin on things. Moisture pooled in her core. Damn.

She looked up to find both Kat and Denise watching her with knowing smiles on their faces. "I can see you are imagining what it would be like," Kat said.

Julia looked at her best friend and nodded.

"Even better than that," Kat said with a satisfied smile as she lifted her drink to her mouth.

"Damn," Julia murmured.

"Oh honey, you have no idea," Kat said.

"Spill," Julia demanded.

"We're going to need more drinks," Denise said.

Chapter Four

The cab dropped the women off in front of the main house and the three stumbled up the stairs giggling. Kat fumbled her keys out of her purse and dropped the entire thing on the porch, the contents scattering in every direction. Giggling, they all dropped to the ground to pick them up. The front door opened, and Julia glanced up to find the doorway filled with hot male bodies. Justin, Kasey, Duncan and Brody all poured on to the porch.

"Looks like you ladies had a fun night," Brody drawled.

Dee stood up and drunkenly glided over to him with an exaggerated hip sway to her as she walked. She trailed her fingers up his chest. She leaned in close. "Those dancers made me horny," her drunk, anything-but-a-whisper voice carried across the deck.

"Gross," Justin groaned, wrinkling his nose at his sister, and making Kasey and Duncan both laugh.

Brody grinned and gave Dee a quick kiss, then turned to the group. "I'm going to take her home and let her objectify me."

Duncan laughed. "Can't say I blame you."

Kat looked up at Justin. "Can I objectify you too?"

Justin grinned. "Anytime, anyplace, baby." He bent down and scooped Kat into his arms.

Kat giggled as she wrapped her arms around his neck. "Night, Jules, I had fun tonight. I'm really glad you decided to stay."

"Me too," Julia replied.

"Go big," Kat called back as Justin carried her into the house.

"What's that about?" Kasey asked as he held out his hand to help Julia up off the porch floor.

She grinned. "You know how it is at girls' night. We get talking."

"Mmm hmm," he said.

"So, when you guys mentioned me joining you, I thought you were joking around. After talking to Kat, I realized maybe you weren't."

Kasey glanced at Duncan then took a step towards her. "We definitely weren't joking."

Holy cow. He was so flippin' hot. She slid closer to him, so their bodies were touching. "I was hoping I could maybe take you up on the offer."

"You want to have a threesome with us?" Kasey asked.

"Very much," Julia replied as she leaned into Kasey's hard body.

Duncan stepped up beside her. "How much have you had to drink tonight?"

She giggled as she thought about all the shots they'd had as the night progressed. She couldn't remember the last time she had drank this much. It surprised her she could still have a conversation. "A lot." She grinned at the men. Normally, she couldn't hold her liquor at all, so she was pretty proud of herself.

"That's what I was afraid of," Duncan murmured.

"What do you mean?" Julia asked.

"Honey, there is nothing we'd like more than to take you to bed and spend hours licking and tasting every inch of your body," Duncan told her.

"Sounds good to me," Julia said as she trailed her fingers up his muscular chest.

Duncan placed his hand on top of hers. "But the first time you come to our bed, it's not going to be when you are completely shitfaced. We need to know this is really what you want."

She stepped back and placed her hands on her hips. "Are you trying to tell me you've never taken a drunk woman to bed?" She scoffed. Hell, most of the sex she'd had in her life had been drunk.

"No, I'm not saying we've never taken a woman home when she's been drinking, but there's a big difference between tipsy and drunk." Duncan tipped her head up and looked her in the eye and smiled. "You are definitely in the drunk category, babe."

"I know, but that's the only reason I'm brave enough to ask," she whined.

Kasey laughed. "The cat's out of the bag now, Jules, so believe me, we aren't going to let you forget you told us you were interested."

"This is stupid. Dee and Kat are just as drunk as I am," she muttered.

Duncan smiled. "I know, babe, but first-time sex and relationship sex are different." He placed a gentle kiss on her lips, and she sighed, slumping towards him. "Mmm," she sighed.

"Jules, believe me, there is nothing I'd rather do than throw you over my shoulder and drag you back to our place to fuck you but," he paused. "You matter to us. We're friends and it would gut me if you regretted it in the morning."

"I'm not going to regret it," she told him. "Kat doesn't."

Duncan laughed. "Good to know, but that situation was a little different as well," Duncan said.

Squealing and giggling noises came from inside the house. Clearly, the objectifying portion of the evening had begun for Kat and Justin. Julia sighed. It didn't look like that was going to play out for her this evening. Guess she'd be hauling out her vibrator.

"Jesus," Kasey groaned.

"Shit, did I say that out loud?" Julia asked as she slapped her hand over her mouth.

"Yep, you sure did." Kasey tightened his hand around her waist and squeezed. "What do you say you come back to our place with us?"

"Really?" Julia asked. She looped her hands behind Kasey's neck and threaded her fingers through his brown hair. "Does this mean you changed your mind?"

He groaned again. "Unfortunately, no. Being honorable fucking sucks." He pulled her against him, and she could feel the outline of his hard cock against her belly.

"Come back to our place. We'll hang out, cuddle up on the bed and watch a movie or something, then in the morning if you are still feeling like this something you want to do, we will be more than happy to fulfill whatever nasty thoughts you've got floating around in that pretty head of yours."

She pressed her hips into his cock, loving the way his hands tightened on her waist, and he dropped his head back and groaned. "Fuck," he muttered.

She glanced at Duncan. His nostrils flared as he looked at her. There was so much heat in his stare she felt it all the way to her clit. Knowing she had this effect on these two sexy men made her feel sexier than she had ever felt in her life. Take that Tyler, you fucker. Two men that were a whole lot hotter than him thought she was worth fucking. But what if she disappointed them?

"Hey where'd you go?" Duncan asked.

"What? Nowhere, I'm right here," she replied.

"You aren't, but that's okay. Let's go back to our place, yeah?" Kasey said.

"Definitely," Julia answered.

Kasey grabbed her right hand and Duncan stepped to her other side and grabbed her left as they made their way towards their cabin. Julia was disappointed she would not live out her fantasy tonight, but they were kidding themselves if they thought she would change her mind. The alcohol might have given her the courage to act on her thoughts, but the desire wasn't going anywhere. If anything, it had just intensified.

She'd known they were good guys in how they had treated her the past couple of weeks, but their integrity tonight? That was a whole other level kind of sweetness. The kind of stuff that made a woman fall in love.

Julia shook her head. She needed to stop those kinds of thoughts. Kasey and Duncan were clearly in love and in a relationship. Anything with her was just about sex. It's not like they could have any kind of relationship with her as well. She needed to remember that and not get all starry-eyed once she had sex with them.

They walked into the cabin. "Movie in bed sound good?" Kasey asked.

Julia looked at the two men. Who was she kidding? She was halfway in love with them both already. Sex was just going to push her over the edge. Lord, she was in trouble. The two men watched her, waiting for an answer. "Movie in bed sounds perfect," she replied. Like Kat said. Go big.

* * * * *

My god it was a million degrees in here. Julia tried to shift but couldn't move. She blinked her eyes open. She was snuggled up against a huge, muscular, naked male back and from behind her she could feel the heat coming off of the body that was spooned up against her back. Oh my. What girl wouldn't want to wake up snuggled between two gorgeous men? No wonder she was so hot. There wasn't an inch of space between the three of them. Who would have thought they'd be snugglers?

Her mind raced back to the night before. Had she really propositioned the men for a threesome? The fact that she was in their bed said she had. Now did she have the courage to go through with it in the cold light of day?

Duncan pressed a kiss against the side of her neck. "I can hear the wheels turning from here, Jules."

She pushed back against him so she could roll onto her back. Turning, she looked into his blue eyes. Lord, even sleep rumpled, the man was beautiful.

He smiled. "Morning," he murmured. He ran his thumb under her eye. "You look like a cute racoon this morning."

Julia yelped and scrambled out of bed. Nope, there was nothing cute about morning after drunken makeup face.

Duncan chuckled. "Where are you going?"

"Men," she muttered as she darted towards the bathroom.

She shut the bathroom door and groaned when she looked at herself in the mirror. She was a hot mess. She washed her face, stole some mouthwash and tried to tame her hair into some semblance of control. After quickly using the facilities, she rested her hands against the bathroom counter and looked at herself in the mirror. Was she really going to do this? Could she do this?

She took a deep breath and exhaled. Yes, she could. She'd be an idiot not to take the guys up on the offer. And she was no idiot. Men like Kasey and Duncan didn't come along very often. Sleeping with one of them would be amazing. She couldn't even wrap her head around what it would be like to be with both of them.

She stood on her tiptoes to look at her body in the mirror, noting the way her hipbones jutted out from her body. Was she too skinny? Kat thought she was. Tyler had always been so critical of her body, watching everything she ate and commenting on any perceived weight gain. Would Kasey and Duncan like what they saw?

She chewed her bottom lip. She closed her eyes and took several deep breaths. She'd left Tyler for a reason. He didn't deserve to have this kind of control over her. Frankly, it pissed her off she was even thinking about him when she should be in the bedroom with Kasey and Duncan. She opened her eyes and stared at herself. *This is your opportunity to be wild and reckless, don't be an idiot. Get in there.*

Fueled by her little pep talk, she opened the bathroom door and looked into the bedroom. Kasey was still fast asleep, but he'd flipped over on to his stomach. Duncan's space was empty. Turning, she walked towards the kitchen and found him making coffee. When she stepped into the room, he slid a mug of steaming coffee across to her. She smiled when she saw he'd remembered to make it the way she liked. Tyler had never bothered to even pour her a cup, let alone remember how she drank it.

"Thank you," she said, and she brought the cup up to her mouth. The sweet smell of caffeine hit her nose and calmed her nerves.

"Sorry you took my teasing wrong this morning. I honestly thought you looked really cute all rumpled up in our bed. I didn't think you'd take it that way."

"It's fine." She laughed. "Here I was thinking you looked so great when you woke up and I looked like a bike tire had run across my face." She shook her head. "Not exactly a look that screams take me."

Duncan's eyes darkened. "Did you want me to take you?"

Her stomach fluttered at the intensity of his stare. "Umm, I wouldn't have minded you wanting to."

Duncan walked around the counter and stopped in front of her. "Believe me honey, I wanted to."

"Really?" she asked.

"Clearly," he said and flipped his hand near his waist, drawing her eyes to the bulge visible beneath his sweatpants. Her eyes lingered on the deep V of his hips and traveled across his muscular abs. She licked her lips. She'd never been with a man with such defined muscles before.

"You might want to stop looking at me like that or we'll be waking up Kase now, not easing into things like we'd planned," Duncan growled.

"You want me that badly?" she asked, taking a step towards him.

He laughed. "You have no fucking idea." He backed her up against the counter. "Kasey and I have discussed fucking you so many times." He pressed his hips into her, and she felt the hard press of his erection against her belly. "All the nasty things we'd like to do to you. How he'd fuck your pussy while you wrapped those full lips around my cock." He rubbed his thumb against her lower lip.

"Open," he told her, and with no thought, she ran her tongue along his thumb and sucked it inside.

Duncan's nostrils flared as he watched her mouth.

"What else would you do to me?" she asked.

"I'd fuck your ass while Dunc fucked your sweet pussy," Kasey's voice said from the entranceway to the kitchen.

Julia looked over at him. His hard cock jutted out from his plaid pajama bottoms. "Wow," Julia murmured.

Kasey stalked over to them. His heated stare bouncing between them. "Looks like I woke up just in time," he said.

"We wouldn't have started without you, don't worry," Duncan said. He turned to Julia. "Now that Kase is up, what are you thinking?"

Jesus, with the way the two men were watching her, she couldn't even speak, let alone form a cognizant thought. She'd never felt so desirable in her life. Wanted. Sexy. Beautiful. Whatever they were offering, she was taking for as long as they were willing to give it.

She leaned against Duncan. The feeling of his hard body pressed up against her back made her shiver. She trailed her finger down Kasey's muscular chest and licked her lips. "I'm thinking I'm all in."

"Fuck yeah," Kasey said as he scooped her up in his arms and carried her to the bedroom.

Julia giggled, the light feeling in her chest easing her concerns about how this would play out.

Kasey set her down on the mattress and followed her down. The mattress dipped as Duncan lay down on her other side.

"So, how does this work, exactly?" Julia asked.

Duncan laughed. "Don't overthink it, Jules."

"I've just never done anything like this before," she whispered. "What if I'm not good at it?"

Duncan pressed a gentle kiss against her lips. "Honey, there's zero possibility you won't be amazing at this. We both want to fuck you. We can be as creative as you want, or we can take it slow and go single file."

"Single file?" Damn, that sounded hot. "Like Kasey fucks me while you are fucking him?" She asked.

A filthy grin split across Duncan's mouth. "That wasn't what I meant at all, but I like the way your mind works." He nodded his head like he was deep in thought. "Yeah, we could definitely do a little train action."

Kasey grunted beside her, drawing their attention to him.

"She knows we fuck, Kase."

"I know we just don't usually—" Kasey said.

Julia looked between the men. "You don't normally fuck each other when you are with women?"

"Nah, Kat's the only women we've ever um," Kasey coughed. "Done anything like that with."

"I thought you guys had threesomes all the time," Julia asked.

"I wouldn't say all the time," Kasey muttered. "We've had few, but we never do anything with each other during them."

"Why not? Wouldn't you enjoy yourselves a lot more if you could also be with each other?"

"Yes," Duncan stated emphatically.

Kasey flipped Duncan the bird.

"Yes, it probably would be better, but it also complicates things, and it's not worth it for a one-night stand," Kasey told her. "Everybody always had a good time." He trailed his fingers down her arm and across her ribcage, making her tremble as goosebumps broke out on her skin. "Besides, there's something to be said for having all of our attention focused on one person. The things we can do to your body with two sets of lips." He pressed a kiss to the crease of her elbow and Duncan did the same to her other arm. She shivered.

"Four hands," he murmured as two sets of hands skimmed across her body. Julia closed her eyes, her senses on overload.

"Two cocks," Kasey whispered against her ear, and she moaned. "Think how good it's going to feel to have all that focused on you."

His hot tongue ran up the side of her neck and he sucked her earlobe into his mouth. Duncan nibbled his way up her neck and proceeded to do the same thing on the other side.

"You might be right," she murmured. "We can test the theory out on you after we are done with me," she said.

"Sounds like a plan," Duncan replied, as he nipped her ear.

When Kasey said nothing, she opened her eyes. He looked back and forth between her and Duncan.

Julia sat up. "What?" she asked.

Kasey shrugged. "I don't know, we've just..." He trailed off.

"You can trust me, Kasey." She took his hand. "Can I ask what's different about the time with Kat? No judgement, I'm just curious."

He sighed. "I don't know. Kat had seen Dunc and I and she thought it was hot."

"You don't think I'd find it just as hot?" she asked. Just the idea of watching them together made her wet. "Believe me, I love the idea."

"Really?" he asked.

"Mmm hmm," she murmured.

"It's just a little different with you. I mean, with Kat, it was just sex. Hell, with all of our activities, it's just sex."

"And it isn't with me?" Julia asked. Her heart beat triple time as she waited for his answer.

"I hope not." He looked at her nervously.

Duncan inhaled audibly beside her.

"You don't want that?" She asked Duncan.

"No, I do. I just am surprised Kase is open to that."

Kasey shrugged. "I mean, it's Jules."

"Yeah, I know," Duncan replied with a smile.

Julia's heart raced as she took in the implication of what they were admitting.

"Have you guys ever had a relationship with a woman?" she asked.

"Not like this, no. We've never really wanted to." Kasey smiled at her. "I don't know. You're different. You aren't really like the buckle bunnies we normally pick up." He shrugged. "You're Kat's best friend. You live here."

Julia looked down at the bedspread. "Oh, I get it, 'cause it would be really awkward if I got all clingy?" she asked.

"What? No. Because you're sexy and sweet, and I know one time will never be enough."

Warmth spread across her chest at what these two men were admitting. They honestly wanted something with her. Julia Cragan. Disposable girlfriend to every other guy she'd ever dated had caught these two amazing men's attention.

But a relationship with two men? God, she couldn't even keep the attention of one man long term. Memories of all the horrible things Tyler had said to her about how boring she was in bed, what a bad lay she was, flashed through her mind. What if they agreed?

"Hey, what's going through that brain of yours?" Duncan asked.

There was no chance she was admitting to him where her thoughts had taken her. "What if the sex sucks?" she asked.

Duncan burst out laughing. "It's sex, Jules. It never sucks."

She snorted. "Speak for yourself."

He waggled his eyebrows. "Believe me, I am." He tipped her chin up. "Honey, if the sex you've had in the past sucked, I'd say you had the wrong partner." He licked his bottom lip as his gorgeous blue eyes scanned her body. "The sex is going to fucking melt your panties off." His gaze lingered on the panties in question. "I can already see how wet you are, and we haven't even started."

Embarrassed, she tried to close her legs, but firm hands pulled her legs back open. "Don't ever be embarrassed about being turned on, honey. I fucking love seeing how wet you already are." His hand trailed up her thigh and his index finger dipped beneath the seam of her panties, and she dropped her head back and moaned.

"Jesus," he groaned. "Jules, the sex is definitely not going to suck."

"Can we stop talking about the sex and start having it?" Kasey asked.

Julia opened her eyes and smiled. "Absolutely.

Duncan peeled off her panties and tossed them on the floor. "Sit up," he ordered as he grabbed the hem of the t-shirt she had slept in and pulled it up and off her body.

"Fuck," Duncan growled. His gaze swept over her body slowly, like a caress. He chewed his bottom lip as his stare lingered on breasts, then traveled lower. The dirtiest grin she'd ever seen split across his face. "This is going to be fun," he said as he grabbed her feet and pulled.

She yelped, then giggled as he dragged her down the bed.

Kasey stared down at her. "Jesus, Jules, you are so fucking beautiful."

She looked up at him and smiled. The way he was looking at her made her feel beautiful. She glanced at Duncan, who looked like he was barely hanging on to his control and a wave of power unlike anything she had ever felt surged through her. She arched her back, pressing her breasts up in the air. "Glad you like what you see," she murmured.

"That's it," Duncan growled. He put both hands on her feet and opened her legs, and moved his muscular body between her feet.

"I thought we were taking this slow," Kasey said, arching his eyebrow at Duncan.

"Sorry Jules, you just looked so — fuck." Duncan roughly ran his hands through his sun- streaked hair as he stared at her core.

She pushed herself up on her elbows and looked first at Duncan, then Kasey. "You don't have to go slow or take things easy with me. I want this as much as you both do. Honestly, it really turns me on to know how badly you want to fuck me."

"That's putting it mildly," Duncan muttered. "But Kasey is right. This is kind of a big deal for you, and I can curb my caveman tendencies a little." He winked. "At least the first time."

Duncan picked up her foot and ran his tongue along her ankle bone. She sucked in a breath at the feel of his hot mouth against her sensitive skin. Kasey tucked his finger beneath her chin and drew her attention towards him. He placed a soft kiss against her lips. "You ready for this?" he asked.

"Absolutely," she told him.

"That's what we want to hear," he told her.

Duncan's tongue slowly trailed up her calf as her leg rested on his shoulder. His beard tickled the inside of leg and she shivered as goosebumps broke out across her skin. Kasey curled his hand against the back of her head, his fingers threading through her hair and with a soft tug, he pulled her head to the angle he wanted.

Good lord, the man could kiss.

The gentle press of his lips against hers was a contrast to the slight pain on her scalp where he guided her by her hair. Kasey's hand teased down her neck and cupped her breast. She moaned as her nipples beaded tightly. Trying to force him to touch her more, she arched her back into his hand. Duncan's tongue swirled against the back of her knee.

Holy shit, she'd never felt anything like this. She didn't know where to focus her attention.

Kasey twisted her nipple gently, and she sucked his tongue into her mouth, eliciting a groan from him.

Duncan ran his tongue up her inner thigh, and she spread her legs wider for him. Holy cow, this was really happening. She was in bed with two amazing men.

Kasey broke the kiss and dragged his teeth down her neck. Shivers ran down her body and moisture pooled in her core. She squirmed on the bed, unable to clamp her legs together to ease the throbbing. Duncan shifted his big body between her legs. He paused and inhaled deeply. "Jesus, you smell good."

"I'll bet she tastes even better," Kasey said.

Duncan's hot tongue swiped across her clit. "Fuck," he growled a moment before his tongue pressed inside her. He fucked her with his tongue while Kasey alternated between licking and sucking her nipples.

"Oh my god," Julia groaned. "Don't stop," she demanded.

"I don't plan to," Duncan told her as he inserted his finger inside her and twisted, hitting a spot she'd only ever been able to hit with her vibrator.

"Oh Jesus," she moaned. She grabbed Kasey's head and pulled him back up so she could kiss him while Duncan continued his assault on her body. Her tongue tangled with Kasey's, and her body climbed higher and higher.

Why had she never slept with a guy with a beard before? Because holy hell, the things Duncan was doing to her body as he rubbed his face back and forth against her wet core. Huge difference between whiskers and a beard. Wow.

Kasey pinched her nipple at the same time Duncan sucked her clit hard, and the orgasm she'd been reaching for slammed into her.

It was too much. She pushed against Duncan's head and tried to close her legs as he continued to lick and suck her sensitive flesh. "Stop, I can't take any more," she said as she pushed her foot against Duncan to get him to stop.

He glanced up and grinned. "You sure? Because I can keep going."

"My god, no," she muttered. "That was." She shook her head. "I don't even." She exhaled. "Wow."

Kasey licked her neck and took her earlobe between her teeth. "That was just the warmup, sweetheart."

Shivers ran down her body, and the muscles in her core contracted. Whether it was a reflex from the orgasm or anticipation, she couldn't say.

Duncan sat up and looked at Kasey, then looked at her. Julia licked her lips, hoping, praying they would kiss. Duncan slid up the bed.

"She tastes fucking amazing," he told Kasey as he placed one hand on the bed beside Julia and the other beside Kasey.

Kasey flicked a glance at her, then back at Duncan. "Yeah?" he asked.

"Yeah. You want a taste?" Duncan asked.

Julia squirmed as she watched the two men staring at each other. The heat in both of their eyes as they looked at each other nearly made her come again.

"Fuck yeah," Kasey said.

Duncan's mouth crashed against Kasey's. There was nothing soft and gentle about this kiss. This was hungry, passionate, and the hottest thing Julia had ever seen.

Without breaking the kiss, Duncan grabbed her hand and pulled it towards his body. She wrapped her hand around his cock, and he groaned. Taking her direction from Duncan, she reached down and wrapped her other hand around Kasey's cock.

She slowly slid her hands up and down both men's cocks. They broke their kiss and turned their attention towards her. She kissed Duncan for the first time. His lips were firmer than Kasey's, but no less skilled. My god these men knew what they were doing.

The kiss broke apart and Duncan looked down at her. "How do you want the first time to be?"

Julia looked at him, then at Kasey. Both men were breathing hard. She could imagine what their muscular bodies would look like moving together and she bit back a moan.

She'd never really been a big talker in the bedroom, but they both seemed to want that from her. "I think I'd like that single file train thing we were talking about."

Duncan grinned. "Yeah, you want to watch me fucking Kasey while he fucks you."

Kasey's cock flexed in her hand when Duncan spoke. He might be shy to admit that was what he wanted too, but his body clearly loved the idea.

Julia nodded. "If that works for you guys."

"It all works for me," Duncan said. He glanced at Kasey. "Kase?"

Kasey's cock flexed again in her hand. He cleared his throat. "Works for me."

Julia wiggled on the bed. "Holy shit," she whispered.

Kasey laughed. "No kidding."

Duncan pressed a kiss to her mouth, then kissed Kasey's lips before he pushed off them both and rolled to the side of the bed. He opened the drawer of the bedside table and removed a box of condoms and a tube of lube.

Duncan tossed a condom to Kasey, who quickly sheathed himself. Kasey moved in between Julia's legs. Kneeling, he leaned over and kissed her. "You sure you are good with all this?"

"I've never been better with anything in my life." She wanted this. She'd never been with a man who checked in like these two did. Tyler always made consent feel like a given. They were in a relationship, so of course if he wanted sex, they'd fuck. Whether or not she was in the mood.

But Kasey and Duncan both checked in regularly every step of the way. Like it mattered to them she was enjoying herself and fully on board. Intellectually, she knew that was, of course, how it always should be, but in her experience, that wasn't the norm. And she really appreciated it. If she was honest, it made her even hotter, which was probably weird, but maybe that's what happened when you'd been in a relationship with dubious consent for a couple of years.

She heard the snap of the lid on the bottle of lube and felt Kasey's body flex against her, as Duncan must have been pouring the lube down his ass. She wrapped her fingers in Kasey's hair and rubbed her pelvis against her cock. She was so wet. He slid easily back and forth against her clit, creating the friction she wanted. He moaned against her mouth at whatever Duncan was doing behind him. Her pussy clenched as she imagined Duncan's fingers prepping Kasey's ass. The idea shouldn't turn her on as much as it did, but holy shit, it really worked for her.

"Ready?" Duncan asked.

Kasey raised up on his arms and looked down at her, a question in his eyes. She smiled. "I'm more than ready."

Kasey grinned back at her, then he kneeled and pulled her hips towards him. His cock stood out proudly from his body. The hard, thick length gave her a moment of pause. His cock was proportionate to his body, but the man was enormous. He was a lot thicker than the guys she'd slept with in the past.

He pressed the head against her, giving her body a chance to adjust to his size. When she relaxed, he pressed further in. Oh my god, he felt huge and freaking amazing. She closed her eyes and arched her hips, pressing so he was fully seated inside her.

"Jesus," Kasey gritted. "You're so tight." Kasey glanced over his shoulder. "Let's get this show on the road because she feels fucking amazing, and I'm not going to last long."

Duncan peeked over Kasey's shoulders and winked at Julia. She grinned back. Duncan's boyish charm added a new fun element that she hadn't known had been missing.

Duncan gripped Kasey's hips and Kasey pulled her with him as he leaned back to allow Duncan access. Kasey's cock surged inside her and seemed to get thicker.

Kasey's breathing grew louder, and Duncan groaned.

Duncan grabbed Kasey's head and turned his face so they could kiss. Their tongues wrapped around each other, and Duncan drove his hips forward, pressing Kasey deeper into her. She moaned. Duncan swiveled his hips, the movement forcing Kasey to match his rhythm as Duncan set the pace for them all. The motion made it feel like she was being fucked by both of them.

The kiss broke apart, and Kasey leaned down and licked her nipple. Fingers flicked her clit. She thought they might have been Duncan's. She closed her eyes and let the sensation take over. The men increased the pace and Kasey bit down on her nipple; the pressure skated between pleasure and pain, and she arched up. Duncan pinched her clit, and all thought left her. There was nothing but feeling. The orgasm ripped through her body and Julia bowed off the mattress as she screamed out her release.

"Fuck yeah, milk my cock, Jules," Kasey groaned.

Duncan growled. He hammered into Kasey, setting an un-relenting pace for Kasey to match with Julia. Kasey groaned as his orgasm hit. Duncan kept driving into Kasey as he chased his own orgasm. Duncan's body continued to cause Kasey to keep fucking Julia, and another orgasm built inside her.

"Hurry up, man, I'm sensitive as fuck," Kasey moaned.

"You'll take it, and you'll like it," Duncan growled.

Kasey's cock flexed inside her, and Julia squeezed her internal muscles. Kasey opened his eyes and looked down at her. "Minx," he said.

Julia smiled. Her second orgasm was just within reach. She reached up and played with her nipples.

"Fuck, that's hot," Duncan said.

Kasey leaned down. "Let me do that for you." He leaned down and sucked her nipple into his mouth, and ground his hips against her. Her orgasm ripped through her at the same time Duncan groaned out his.

Kasey dropped his head against her neck, his breathing shallow and hard. She could feel Duncan breathing from his place against Kasey's back. Julia opened her eyes and found Duncan's blue eyes looking back at her.

"You good?" he asked.

"Once I gain the ability to think, I'll let you know," she replied.

"Sounds like we did a good job then," he teased.

"I don't want to squish Jules," Kasey said as he pushed back. His powerful muscles flexed as he took Duncan's body with him.

Duncan dropped onto the mattress on her right and Kasey laid down on her left. Sandwiched between the two men, Julia sighed. She had never felt better. Whatever this turned out to be between them was already better than any fantasy she could ever imagine.

Duncan rolled on his back and scratched his belly. "I need a shower."

"Me too." Kasey trailed his fingers down her hip. "You want to join?"

They were like freaking energizer bunnies if they thought she was ready to go again already. "Nope. You guys go. I'm just going to close my eyes for a minute."

"We'll be quick," Kasey said as he hopped out of bed.

"No rush. I know you probably want a minute for yourselves."

"What are you talking about, woman? If we were looking for that, we wouldn't have asked you to join us." Duncan pressed a kiss against her lips, then pushed out of bed. "Trust me, we'll be quick. I've got plans for you today."

She smiled to herself and closed her eyes.

For the first time in longer than she could remember, she felt desirable, and more than that, she didn't feel lonely.

Chapter Five

Kasey walked back into the bedroom and paused when he saw Julia lying in bed, her arm across her eyes, the sheet draped across her hip. My god, she was so beautiful.

"Hey sleeping beauty," he said.

Julia dragged her hand off her face. "I'm not asleep, but I think you guys killed me."

Kasey laughed. "You wouldn't be talking, babe."

"Mmm," she grunted.

"Why don't I go make us something to eat so you can fuel up and get your strength back."

Julia pushed to her side. "I can help."

"Nah, that's fine, I've got it." What he really wanted to do was climb back into bed with her, but clearly, she needed a bit of a break.

"I want to," Julia replied. She pulled the sheet with her as she sat up on the bed and scanned the room. She eyed the pile of clothes on the floor.

Kasey walked over to the dresser and grabbed a fresh t-shirt from his drawer and handed it to her. "Here, that might be more comfortable than what you had on last night."

"Thanks," she replied, taking the worn t-shirt from him.

"Finally, it sounds like Duncan's done in the shower. Justin called just before he climbed into the shower, so he had to take the call. But now that he's done, let's get cracking in the kitchen so we can eat."

He grabbed her hand and pulled her off the bed. His attention immediately snagged on her pert breasts. He took the shirt from her and pulled it over her head. The sooner he got her covered, the sooner he could get his mind off fucking her again. The shirt engulfed her body, nearly coming to her knees. It should have looked ridiculous on her. Instead, he couldn't imagine anything sexier.

"So, what are we making?" Julia asked as she leaned against the kitchen counter.

"Well, I have two things in my breakfast repertoire, so your choices are bacon and eggs or waffles."

"You can make waffles?" Julia asked. "Well, clearly, the answer is always going to be waffles." Julia walked towards the fridge. "Any chance you have some fruit or whipped cream."

Kasey's mind immediately began picturing Julia spread out on the kitchen table with whipped cream strategically covering her body. "No whipped cream, but it's definitely going on the next shopping list," he told her.

Julia turned around to look at him. Her eyes darkened as a blush rose up her cheeks. She licked her lips. "I'll make sure I pick some up," she murmured.

Kasey stalked towards Julia, and she backed up until she was pressed against the fridge. "Umm Kasey?" Julia said.

"What?" he replied as he caged her in against the fridge.

"I thought we were making breakfast," she said.

He leaned in and ran his tongue up the length of her neck. "I want something else for breakfast."

"Oh." She shuddered out a breath. "Ok, sounds good," she sighed.

Kasey grabbed her by the hips, picked her up, and set her on the edge of the kitchen counter. The height put her exactly where he wanted her. He pressed his hips against her core. He could feel the heat of her through his sweatpants. He made eye contact with Julia and held her stare until she shifted her hips against him, seeking more contact. With a smile, he dropped to his knees on the kitchen floor without breaking eye contact with her. Julia licked her lips and shifted her hips closer to the edge of the counter.

Kasey placed a kiss at her ankle then slowly kissed a path up her calf. Julia's legs parted, and she placed her other foot on his shoulder, baring herself to him. He couldn't wait to bury his face in her pussy. He hadn't had the chance earlier.

He licked a trail up her inner thigh. When he reached the top, he inhaled deeply. The scent of Julia filled his senses. She smelled fucking amazing. He swiped his tongue along her slit. And tasted even better.

Julia moaned at the first contact of his mouth on her pussy. She leaned back on her elbows and threaded her fingers through his hair. He swirled his tongue around her clit, enjoying the way her body rhythmically moved against his face as she tried to direct him where she wanted. He put his hands under her and lifted her ass off the counter to get the angle he wanted, and Julia pulled his head against her firmly. Kasey grinned to himself. Guess the new position worked for her.

He continued to lick and suck at her clit, taking his cues from the mewling sounds and hip thrusts from Julia. He loved seeing her like this, wild and turned on, taking what she wanted from him. This was not the self-conscious woman that had arrived at the ranch. He inserted his finger inside her and she clamped her legs tightly around his ears as she thrust up towards him.

The little noises Julia made grew louder as he fucked her with his finger.

"Jesus, Kasey. Right there, right there, right there," she moaned.

He swirled his tongue around her clit, then sucked it firmly into his mouth and she screamed out her release. Her inner muscles clamping down on his finger as her thighs squeezed his head.

"Holy shit," Julia muttered as she dropped her legs onto his shoulders.

Kasey placed a kiss on her inner thigh and pushed himself up to standing.

He glanced over at Duncan, who was leaning against the back of the couch, watching them. His gray sweatpants tented by his arousal.

"That was fucking hot," Duncan said.

Julia pushed up to seated. She glanced at Duncan, then Kasey, then back to Duncan. "I don't know the rules here. Is this okay?"

Duncan pushed off the couch and walked over to Kasey. He cupped the back of his head and pulled him in for a hard, hot kiss. His tongue aggressively tangled with Kasey's, making his cock pulse with need. When he pulled away, Kasey was breathing hard, but then Duncan always had that effect on him.

Duncan looked at Julia. "Is waking up to Kasey eating you out in the kitchen and then me being able to taste you on his tongue when I take my morning kiss, okay?" He glanced at Kasey, and the heat in his eyes made Kasey's dick twitch. "Yeah, that's definitely okay."

"Okay, good," Julia murmured. "I don't really know what we are doing here."

Duncan put his hands around Julia's hips and scooped her off the counter. She squealed as she wrapped her legs around his waist. "What are you doing?" she giggled.

Duncan set her down on the kitchen table. "The counter was too small for what I wanted. What we are going to be doing here is finishing what you two started." He kissed Julia on the lips. "If I know Kase, he's dying to fuck you and I want those pretty lips of yours wrapped around my dick. Does that work for you?"

Julia nodded her head vigorously.

Kasey reached into the kitchen drawer and pulled a sleeve of condoms out of the drawer. He pulled one off as he walked over to them. He pushed his sweatpants down and fisted his cock, enjoying the way Duncan and Julia both watched him hungrily.

He pulled Julia's t-shirt up and off her head and tossed it on the table. Placing a hand in the center of her chest, he pushed her down, so she was lying spread out on the table. He grabbed her hips and pulled her to the edge of the table. He placed himself at the entrance to her body. Heat engulfed his cock. He looked at Julia and widened her legs and shifted her hips. She was so wet the movement pulled him just inside. Kasey groaned and thrust his hips forward, seating himself fully inside. Julia arched her back off the table.

Duncan pushed his sweatpants down and his cock sprang free. Kasey watched as Julia wrapped her hand around the long, hard length and gently guided him towards her mouth. She swirled her tongue around the head and Duncan sucked in a breath. Kasey couldn't take his eyes off Julia, licking and sucking Duncan's cock. Kasey thrust his hips in time with the movement of Duncan's hips thrusting as he fucked Julia's mouth. Kasey reached his hand down and swirled his fingers around Julia's clit, and she moaned.

"You two better hurry up because I'm not going to last long at this rate," Duncan growled. Julia smiled around Duncan's cock, and the teasing glimmer in her eyes nearly brought Kasey to his knees. They'd done that, they'd brought that out in her. Fuck, he felt like he could conquer the world. Julia might not be fully healed, but she had come a long way in the few short weeks they'd known her.

He thrust into her and pinched her clit between his fingers. Whatever Julia did with her mouth made Duncan groan. "Fuck, Jules, I'm going to come." Duncan tried to pull back, but Julia grabbed his cock with her hand and forced him to stay. "Jesus," Duncan groaned.

Julia wiped her lips, then looked back at Kasey. He held her stare as he fucked her. Duncan sucked her nipple as Kasey shifted his hips to change the angle, hoping to hit where she needed. Julia gasped. "Don't stop," she told them.

Duncan slid down and pushed Kasey's fingers out of the way as he swiped his tongue along Julia's clit. Julia screamed out her release. Her back arched so far off the table he could barely hold on to her, and Kasey dug his fingers into her hips as he held her in place so he could fuck her. Duncan's fingers cupped his balls and Kasey roared out his own release.

Kasey leaned roughly against the table. He sucked in several breaths as he tried to gain his balance.

What was it about this woman? He and Duncan had had lots of threesomes, and he'd never felt like this afterwards. This feeling? Holy shit, this was what had been missing. He opened his eyes and met Duncan's knowing smile. Guess he wasn't the only one feeling it, but what the hell did it mean? It's not like this could be forever.

Kasey looked at Julia spread out on the table with her eyes closed. She looked like she had fallen asleep. He smiled and looked over at Duncan.

"Well, what were you two planning to make to eat before you got distracted?" Duncan asked. Kasey tried to make eye contact with Duncan, but it was like a shutter had closed. Kasey could no longer read what he was thinking. Maybe, like him, Duncan was wondering how long this would last.

*****

"Spill," Kat demanded when she walked into the kitchen.

Julia pushed herself up off the floor, where she sat surrounded by Tupperware containers.

"How is it possible that not a single one of these containers seems to have a matching lid?" Julia shook her head as she looked at the pile before her. "I think it would just be easier to junk them all and start again."

"Are you seriously talking to me about Tupperware right now?" Kat asked.

"What? It's true. How does that cupboard not drive you crazy?" Julia replied.

"Oh, my god, stop. Stop avoiding the conversation," Kat growled.

"What conversation? I'm the housekeeper slash cook in this house, and I can't find a single freaking piece of Tupperware that will work to store food. I'm going to have to go to Dee's house and see if somehow the matching pieces ended up there." Julia shook her head. "Tupperware and freaking socks, man, the bane of my existence."

"How's the Tupperware situation at your new place with the boys?" Kat asked with a smirk.

Julia laughed. "Subtle, Kat, real subtle."

"Well, come on. I haven't had a chance to really talk to you about how things are going with the guys."

"They're good. They're clean. It only took a couple of discussions to get them to leave the toilet seat down, so all in all, they make good roommates," Julia replied.

"Roommates?" Kat asked and raised her eyebrow. "Is that all they are?"

"Well, they are my roommates." She bit back a grin. "But we might all sleep in the same room."

"I knew it," Kat squealed.

"What did you know?" Julia asked.

"I knew you were interested in a three-way with them when we went drinking that night." Kat rested her chin on her hands and leaned towards Julia.

"So how long did it take you to break them down and get them to forget about their conscience."

"What do you mean, forget about their conscience?" Julia asked.

Kat shrugged. "I know the guys were both interested in starting something up with you, but they were worried about whether you were ready to date after everything."

"How did you know they were interested in dating me?"

"Justin mentioned it." Kat stood up and walked to the fridge. "We need wine."

"It's the middle of the workday." Julia laughed.

"My husband owns the joint. I think we're good." Kat shrugged.

She poured two glasses and handed one to Julia. "Let's go sit on the couch. It's more comfortable."

Julia followed Kat into the spacious living room. She loved this room with the big fireplace and comfy couches. It was rustic and lived in. The quality of the furniture clearly spoke of Justin having money, but everything in the room felt like him, down to earth and chill. It was a room you could put your feet up on the couch and no one would give you the side eye. It had only been a little over a month, but already Julia felt like she had a place here, like she belonged.

She dropped down on the couch and curled her feet up underneath herself.

"Honestly, I'm kind of surprised the guys agreed to a three-way. I kind of had the impression from Justin that both guys were interested in something more," Kat told her.

Julia smiled as she pictured the way the relationship was developing between the three of them. "I think they want something more. We're trying to figure things out and how this might all work."

"Seriously," Kat said, wide-eyed. "Is that what you want? You'd be happy having a long-term relationship like that? It seems like it could be complicated."

"I'm not naïve enough to think this could last forever. I mean, look at them. They are both fucking beautiful and two of the sweetest guys I've ever met. Before meeting them, I didn't know guys like this really existed. It sure as hell wasn't my experience with men." She sighed. "Truthfully, I keep expecting them to realize they don't need me at all."

"What do you mean, they don't need you?" Kat asked.

"I don't know. I mean, the connection between Kasey and Duncan is unreal. Not only are they obviously best friends, but my god, the heat between them."

Kat chuckled. "Yeah, they are pretty smoking together," she said as she fanned her face. "But what does that have to do with them not needing you? I've seen the way they've looked at you the past few weeks and that was before they had a chance to get their hands on you. There's no way things aren't smoking between all of you."

"Oh, no, they are, Jesus, are they ever." She placed her hand against her chest as her heart kicked up a notch, thinking about what it was like between them. "It's just, I don't know that us all being together like this is sustainable. I mean, how would that work exactly?" She looked over at Kat. "And there's no way either of them would choose me over each other, and I couldn't choose one of them." She sighed. "I'm crazy about both of them. Hell, I think I was half in love with them both before I ever slept with them. The way they've treated me since I got here has been amazing."

Kat laughed. "Yeah, once Kasey realized you didn't plan to make off with the family china."

Julia grinned. "His first impression was a bit rough, but I understood it. He didn't know me from Adam. Why would he trust me? But he's more than made up for it. He's so sweet and Duncan is just — God, he's just so fun and easygoing until..." She sighed as she thought about how take-charge he could be. Who would have thought?

"Kinda different in the bedroom?" Kat added.

"Yeah, and my god, is it hot." Julia took a sip of her wine and leaned back on the couch. "It's a complicated situation and

I'm trying not to do what I normally do and overthink it. I'm just going to enjoy this for as long as they want me."

"And if they don't want to let you go?" Kat asked.

"Then I'd feel very blessed." But that would not happen. Things would get complicated, and they'd chose each other. The love between the men was tangible. If things fell apart, she'd be the odd one out and it would destroy her. She took another sip of wine as she thought about what she had with Kasey and Duncan.

"You got quiet there. What are you thinking about?" Kat asked.

"I'm thinking how it's worth the risk. I wouldn't do anything to come between Kasey and Duncan. What they have with each other is so special. I'm just hoping we can figure out a way to make this work for all of us." She looked at her childhood friend and smiled. "And in the meantime, my god, do they know what they are doing in the bedroom."

Kat giggled. "I hear ya. There is just something about a work-hardened body and those calloused hands. Mmm." Kat sighed.

"Their muscles are ridiculous. That sexy hip vee they both have. Holy shit, I just want to lick it."

Kat giggled and brought her wineglass up to her lips.

Julia slapped her hand across her mouth. "Sorry, over-share."

"Don't apologize. I know exactly what you are talking about. I can't keep my tongue away from that on Justin, either."

"The guys I've known did not have bodies like these," Julia told her.

"It was a new experience for me, too. Plus, the stamina that goes along with it." Kat waggled her eyebrows and Julia snorted.

The front door opened, and Justin pushed through the doorway, followed by Kasey and Duncan.

"Look at you two slackers," Justin said as he sat down on the arm of Kat's chair. "Day drinking?" Justin shook his head.

"Sorry, I know I'm supposed to be working," Julia said as she quickly pulled her feet off the couch and stood up.

"Sit back down, Jules. I couldn't care less that you guys are hanging out," Justin told her. "There's a storm rolling in, so we are wrapping up early, anyway. The guys just came in to get you and bring you home before it hits."

Julia looked at Kasey and Duncan. Duncan stood with his feet apart, thumbs hooked in his front pockets, drawing her eye right to his crotch. Julia's nipples tightened. She glanced up, and Duncan gave her a cocky wink as he mouthed. "Busted."

"What were you ladies talking about when we walked in?"

Julia said nothing at the same time Kat said. "Your bodies."

Kasey coughed. "Sorry what?"

"We were talking about what great bodies you all have." Kat trailed her hand down Justin's forearms. "Muscles for days and how yummy they are."

Justin laced his fingers with Kat's and brought her hand up to his mouth. He placed a kiss on her knuckles. "You know what else is yummy?" Justin said quietly.

"Dude, we can all hear you." Duncan laughed.

"Get the fuck out of my house. I have plans for my wife," Justin told them.

Kat giggled and gave a little wave to the three of them as they walked towards the door. Julia loved seeing Kat so happy. As she followed the men towards their own place, she smiled. For the first time in her life, she felt like she had a real chance for that kind of happiness, too.

"I bought whipped cream when I was at the grocery story," Julia called over her shoulder as she made her way down the porch steps.

Chapter Six

Her foot had barely hit the bottom rung when she was swept up into muscular arms. The wide span of the back told her it was Kasey's shoulder she was slung over like a fire victim.

Julia giggled. "I take it you are on board with my idea?"

A smack landed on her right butt cheek, and she squealed. "Ouch, Duncan," she laughed.

"How'd you know it was me?" he asked.

"Because Kasey is too much of a gentleman to smack my ass that hard," she teased.

"Yeah, that's true," Duncan agreed.

"Hey, I'm not always a nice guy," Kasey grumbled.

Julia rubbed Kasey's back while hanging upside down over his shoulder. "Yes, you are, sweetie."

Kasey set her down on her feet inside the front door of their place.

She looked at him and smiled at the little pout on his rugged face. Cupping his cheek with her palm, she said, "It's not a bad thing. I like that you both are so different in the bedroom."

"How are we so different?" he asked.

"I don't know." She shrugged. "I mean, look at you, Kasey. You're huge. You look like you could break a person in half without even trying, but in the bedroom, you are always so sweet and gentle with me. Looking at you, I would never have expected it."

She glanced over at Duncan. "And Duncan is so laid back, always joking, but you get him in the bedroom and he's so focused and in control, telling us both what to do." She smiled at the two men. "You both are so different, but together — My god, it just works."

Duncan stepped up behind her. "Then how about we take off that shirt so Kasey and I can do our best work."

He ran his tongue up the side of her neck as his fingers hooked on the bottom of her shirt and pulled it over her head. He didn't pull it all the way off, leaving her arms trapped in the fabric of the sleeves.

Julia squirmed to pull her arms free. Duncan's powerful hands held her wrists captive behind her back. "Stop squirming and let us play."

"Kase, why don't you grab that whipped cream Julia was tormenting us about?" Duncan suggested.

He walked her over to the back of the couch and pressed against her mid-back until she was bent over across the top. Her arms tied behind her back, her ass sticking out. Duncan ran his hand down her bare back and across her ass cheek.

"Let's get these jeans off," he told her.

She shivered as his fingers slowly peeled her jeans down her legs. She felt so vulnerable and exposed, with her ass on display in the cold light of day.

"Step out," Duncan told her as he picked up her leg to pull her foot free of her jeans. He tossed the jeans to the side and leaned back on his haunches.

"Your ass," he muttered, followed by a sharp nip on her ass cheek.

"Did you just bite me?" she asked.

"Sure did." He nipped the other cheek. "I can't help myself. Your ass is so fucking sweet." He stood up and swatted her ass cheek hard.

She moaned. What was wrong with her? Getting her ass slapped shouldn't turn her on so damned much, but every time Duncan swatted her ass, it was like there was a lightning rod attached to her clit.

She heard Kasey's footsteps come up beside her, and she turned her head to look at him.

His work-roughened fingers swept across her ass cheeks in a gentle caress. "He's not kidding. Jesus, the things I want to do to your ass," he muttered.

She twisted on the back of the couch to get a better look at him. "Like what?"

"Fuck it for one," Kasey told her.

Her eyes widened.

"You'd like that, wouldn't you?" he asked.

Duncan's hand trailed up her inner thigh as he leaned against her side.

"Would you like us both to fuck you at the same time, Jules? One of us in your ass, the other in that hot pussy?" Duncan whispered in her ear.

She shuddered as a wave of lust shivered down her spine, followed by a ripple of unease. Part of her loved the idea of both of them fucking her at the same time. She stood up and turned around so she was facing them both. She looked at Kasey standing before her, so huge and strong, then at Duncan's long, lean frame. How would this work? They were both so big there was no way. The logistics didn't make sense. She chewed her bottom lip.

"I'm not sure the first time I'm fucked in the ass should also be a double team kind of thing," she told them, laughing nervously.

Duncan's eyes darkened even further. She wouldn't have thought it was possible for him to look more aroused than he did before, but he did. "You've never done anal?" he asked.

"No." She shook her head.

"Why not?" he asked as he trailed a hand down her spine. His hand caressed her ass cheek as he held her stare.

"I don't know. It kind of scares me a bit," she whispered.

"Why does it scare you?" he asked.

"What if it hurts?"

Duncan made a face that made her think pain was a real possibility. She glanced at Kasey. He smiled kindly. "It can hurt a little at first if you don't take your time." He cupped her cheek in his big, calloused palm. "But it's a good kind of hurt."

"What the fuck's a good hurt?" she scoffed.

Duncan laced his fingers through her hair and pulled slightly. Her eyes widened as the pain and his control over her shot an arrow of lust through her.

"That's a good kind of hurt," Duncan told her. He bent and swirled his tongue around her nipple, then bit it firmly. She moaned as moisture pooled in her core.

"So's that," he whispered.

"Oh," she sighed.

Kasey turned her head back towards him. "How about we save the two of us fucking you for another day and just start with Duncan fucking you in the ass while I eat you."

Julia looked at Duncan. His nostrils flared as he watched her intently. His muscles coiled tight as he looked at her like he wanted to devour her. She glanced nervously at Kasey. Holy shit, was she ready for this? She chewed her bottom lip. Maybe they should just have normal sex and work up to this whole butt thing.

"Trust me, he'll be gentle. He knows what he's doing." Kasey pressed a soft kiss against her lips. "He's the only person I've been with that way, and you couldn't ask for anyone better."

Duncan pressed his body up against her side, drawing her attention back to him. "Trust me, Jules, we'll make this so good for you," he told her.

"I do trust you," she whispered.

"Good." He leaned in and pressed his lips against her mouth. Taking her hand, he pulled her towards the bedroom. "Kase, bring the whipped cream," he ordered.

"We're still going to do that?" she asked.

"Fuck yeah," Duncan growled.

"Plus, it will help you relax. You'll be so turned on, you'll be begging him to fuck your ass when we're done with you," Kasey told her.

"Oh my," she sighed.

Julia followed Duncan into the bedroom. She lay down on the bed, while Duncan peeled his shirt over his head and tossed it in the corner of the room.

Kasey set the whipped cream on the bedside table. He hooked his hand in the back of his shirt and pulled it over his head one handed. She shifted her body until she could watch the two men undress.

"So, were you and Kat really talking about our bodies when we got there?" Duncan asked.

"Yep," she licked her lips as she looked at both men standing before her with their shirts off, their jeans riding low on their hips.

"I mean, look at you two. Your muscles are insane," she said. Her eyes lingered on the vee cut above Kasey's waistband.

Duncan walked over to Kasey and trailed his hand along the ridges of his abdominal muscles. "He does have really nice abs," Duncan said, causing Kasey to blush.

Kasey swatted his hand. "Stop it."

Duncan looked at Julia. "You want me to stop?"

She shook her head. "God no."

"What do you want, Jules?" Duncan asked her.

"I want to watch you undress each other and kiss and then you can come over here to me." She propped herself up on the pillow on the bed so she could really enjoy the show in front of her.

Duncan winked at her. "With pleasure."

Duncan placed himself at Kasey's back and kissed the side of his neck. His fingers hooked in the waistband of Kasey's jeans and he slowly undid the button. Duncan's eyes never left Julia's face as he eased Kasey's jeans down his body.

Julia's nipples beaded tightly as she watched the sensual display in front of her. Who knew how much she liked to watch? Tyler had tried to get her to watch porn with him, and it had left her cold. But this? Watching Kasey and Duncan, nothing about it made her cold. She clamped her thighs together as Duncan shoved Kasey's black boxer briefs down his thighs. He grabbed Kasey's thick cock in his hands and firmly stroked it. Kasey spun around. His arm banded around Duncan's neck as he pulled him into a rough kiss. Their tongues tangled as Kasey urgently fought with Duncan's jeans and shoved them down his legs. The men broke apart from their kiss, breathing hard.

They looked over at her, then back at each other. The two men shared a look, then stalked towards the bed. Julia swallowed as she tried to fill her lungs with air. "Holy shit," she muttered.

Kasey picked up the whipped cream from the bedside table. Duncan grabbed her by the ankles and pulled her down the bed, so she was no longer sitting partially upright.

Kasey held the can of whipped cream above her right nipple. The first cold spray against her skin made her gasp as her nipple tightened painfully. Duncan's hot mouth quickly sucked up the whipped cream. The contrast between the cold whipped cream and his hot mouth made her squirm on the mattress. Duncan's hand clamped down on her hip.

"Hold still so we can enjoy ourselves," he ordered.

Kasey painted her body with a trail of whipped cream that Duncan followed with his tongue. As they continued to paint and lick her body, she desperately tried to stay still, but she couldn't. She panted as her body fought to get what she needed.

"Oh my god, quit teasing me, you two," she whined.

"On your knees," Duncan ordered.

Holy shit, this was happening. She flipped over onto her knees and nervously looked over her shoulder at Duncan. He placed a kiss against her lower back. "Trust us," he told her.

Kasey lay down on his back and slid his body underneath Julia. She glanced down at him, and he grinned. "Feel free to enjoy the position as well," he said as he waggled his eyebrows.

She laughed. "What is it about guys and the ol' 69?" she asked.

"Is that a real question?" Kasey asked. "I mean come on. My dick is getting sucked while I'm eating your pussy. There is no negative in that scenario."

"Well, when you put it that way," Julia laughed.

The sound of the lube cap snapping open drew her attention back to Duncan. Cool liquid dripped down her ass, and she sucked in a breath. Every muscle in her body tensed. *Oh boy, here we go.*

"This will work best if you can try to relax a bit, Jules," he told her.

"Right, relax as you empale me with your monster cock," she said.

"Well, thanks for the compliment, darlin', but we both know it's not a monster." He kissed the middle of her spine. "Be glad it's me and not Kasey."

She glanced down to where Kasey's thick cock stood proudly, begging for attention. A bead of pre-cum dripped from the tip. "Good point," she murmured. It took some adjustment for her pussy to accept Kasey, and it was used to being fucked. There was no way her virgin ass was ready for that thing.

Duncan sheathed himself in a condom and tossed the wrapper to the side. Firm hands gripped her hips, and a finger eased between her cheeks, making her gasp. "Relax, Jules, we'll ease into this," Duncan told her.

Kasey swirled his fingers around her nipples, and she moaned as Duncan eased his finger into her ass. "Oh my god," she groaned.

"Feel good?" Duncan asked.

"Um... yeah..." He expected her to talk at a time like this?

Duncan chuckled as he continued to move his finger. He added another finger, and she felt the burning as he scissored his fingers inside her.

"You still okay?" he asked.

"I'm good," she told him. She now understood what they had been talking about when he said it hurt so good. There was a slight pain as he moved his fingers, but the sensation was unlike anything she had ever felt. Maybe it was the forbiddenness of it all, but holy shit.

Kasey's tongue trailed up her inner thigh, and she widened her legs. Duncan removed his fingers, and she felt him place his cock against her back entrance. She took a deep breath.

"Relax, Jules," he told her.

"Easier said than done," she muttered.

Kasey's hot breath exhaled against her clit as he laughed. "Let me see if I can help with that," he told her.

Kasey's tongue swirled around her clit, and she moaned. She dropped her head down. Her gaze landed on Kasey's cock, and she smiled to herself. She swirled her tongue around the head of his cock, and he grunted against her pussy.

Julia sucked his cock into her mouth as Duncan pressed against the outer ring of her ass. "Relax, Jules, and press back," he told her.

Kasey sucked her clit hard, and she moaned around his cock as Duncan fully seated himself inside her. Holy shit. Pain burned through her ass, quickly followed by a jolt of raw carnal lust. The primal urgency to move shocked her. He was too deep, yet not deep enough at the same time. She didn't know what she needed or wanted.

Duncan's hand clamped around her hips. "We've got you," he told her.

How the hell could he have her when she didn't know what she needed?

But then he started moving as Kasey licked and slurped at her clit, and she got it. Holy shit did she get it. Why had no one told her she could feel like this before?

"Jesus," she moaned. She opened her eyes and realized she had completely forgotten about sucking Kasey's cock. She opened her mouth and sucked him in deep. She allowed the pace that Duncan set to dictate her own.

Kasey inserted his fingers inside her as he licked her clit. Holy shit, she was going to explode if she didn't come soon. She sucked his cock harder, and his hips bucked off the mattress.

All she could hear was licking and slurping noises, grunts, and groans. She didn't know what noises belonged to who, and she didn't care. The orgasm built inside her. The strength of what was building made her suck in a breath. She pulled off Kasey's cock as she lost coordination. It was too much. She couldn't take it.

"You can and you will," Duncan growled.

She didn't realize she'd spoken out loud. "I don't think I can," she muttered.

"Yes, you can, Jules, just let go," he ordered

Kasey pinched her nipple hard as he continued to fuck her with his fingers and lick her clit. She felt so full, with Duncan in her ass and Kasey's fingers. She couldn't imagine how she would ever take them both if she felt like this now. Kasey slurped her clit hard, and she screamed as they dragged out her orgasm.

Gasping to catch her breath, she dropped her head onto Kasey's belly as Duncan continued to drive into her. She felt Kasey slide a little further beneath her, then Duncan groaned loudly. "Fuck, Kase," he growled.

She didn't know exactly what Kasey was doing, but from the sound of Duncan's moans, it was good. She picked up her head and sucked Kasey's cock back into her mouth, and he moaned. "Jesus, Jules, your mouth," Kasey gritted out.

She continued to suck his cock. She cupped his balls and tickled her finger just behind his sac.

Duncan's hands gripped her hips hard as he growled out his orgasm. He held her still as he finished, then collapsed against her back. She continued to suck Kasey's cock as his balls pulled up tight, letting her know how close he was.

"I'm going to come, Jules," he told her.

She smiled around his cock and took him deeper, sucking down his orgasm.

They collapsed in a heap on the bed with limps going every which way, but no one seemed to have the energy to move. She felt a hand caress her back, but she didn't know who it belonged to, and she didn't care.

How had she gotten so lucky to find these men?

That was the last conscious thought she had before she drifted off to sleep.

Chapter Seven

Kasey hung up the phone and turned around. Duncan and Julia watched him expectantly.

"My Mom just wanted to double check I was coming home next weekend for Lisa's graduation."

"Who's Lisa?" Julia asked.

"My little sister." He couldn't believe his baby sister was graduating from college already.

"Tell her congrats," Duncan replied.

"What do you mean, tell her? You know my mom expects you to be there."

Duncan shrugged. "You sure you want me to come?"

"Of course, why wouldn't I? You too, Julia. I was telling my parents all about you and they're looking forward to meeting you."

Julia beamed back at him. "Really, you want me to come too?" She glanced over at Duncan, then back at Kasey.

He wrapped his arm around her shoulders and placed a kiss on top of her head. "You can be my date."

Her brow wrinkled with confusion. "What about Duncan?"

"Nope, he's all yours at family functions," Duncan replied.

"What do you mean?" Julia looked back and forth between the two men.

"I mean, as far as Kasey's family is concerned, he and I are just friends."

"But you guys have been together forever."

"Yeah, funny huh?" Duncan scoffed. He pushed away from the table. "I've got work to do," he said and, without a second look back, he left the kitchen.

Julia shifted, so Kasey was forced to look her in the eye. "Why don't your parents know about Duncan?"

He shrugged.

"No, come on, don't brush me off. Why haven't you told them?"

"I don't know. My parents aren't real liberal, you know? Dunc knows that and he's fine with it."

Julia glanced towards the door. "You sure?"

He followed her stare. No, he wasn't sure, but what was he supposed to do? Pushing away the feelings of doubt, he turned back to Julia. "So, how about it? Will you be my official girlfriend for the weekend?"

Julia smiled. "Just for the weekend, or will I still be your girlfriend when we get home?"

Kasey stepped in close and wrapped his arms around her waist. "Do you even have to ask that question?"

Julia looked towards the door when Duncan had left. "I don't know, do I?"

Kasey dropped his arms from Julia's waist and stepped away from her. "It's not the same thing at all, Jules."

"No? How's it different?"

"No," Kasey growled. "Duncan and I have an understanding. He knows I care about him and why I can't tell my family."

"He seemed a bit upset about it," Julia pressed.

God, why did they have to discuss this? He and Duncan had been cruising along for years doing what they were doing without discussing things like the future and what this all meant. Duncan understood why they were, how they were, why couldn't Julia be the same? "It means I'm not willing to talk to my parents about the fact that Duncan and I fuck, okay?"

"Come on, Kasey, don't play that way with me. You do a hell of a lot more than fuck."

"Yeah, and Duncan knows that, but I don't have to tell the entire world, do I?"

"Not the entire world, no, but maybe your family?"

Kasey thought about the reaction he would get from his parents if he told them he was in a relationship with Duncan and Julia. Yeah, no, there was zero chance of that happening.

"We only see my family a few times a year, so it's no big deal. We both have this thing down pat."

"Okay, you know him better than I do."

Kasey wrapped his arms around her waist again and pulled her against him. "It's going to be fine. I promise. We'll all go, and we'll have a great time." He placed a kiss against her mouth, loving the way she melted into his body. "I'm looking forward to introducing you to my family."

Julia smiled shyly at him. "I'm looking forward to meeting them, too."

Kasey rested his chin against the top of Julia's head. He was puzzled by Duncan's reaction. He was normally so laid back and chill about everything. Discussing their relationship had never been anyone else's business, and Duncan had always been fine with that. So, what was today about?

Julia wrapped her arms tighter around his waist and squeezed him, and Kasey responded instinctively. Shit, that was probably Duncan's problem. Kasey would be able to touch Julia and have this with her at his parent's house and Duncan couldn't. He needed to talk to him about that before they left.

*****

The following weekend, the three of them piled into Kasey's truck with Julia in the backseat.

"So, what's the plan for the weekend?" Julia asked. She couldn't wait to meet Kasey's family, to be given a glimpse at a different side of the man she was dangerously close to falling in love with.

"Tomorrow afternoon is my sister's grad ceremony, so we'll all go to that, then head back to my parent's place for a BBQ with all the friends and family." Kasey shifted in his seat. "When I'm home, I usually go to church on Sunday morning with my folks, then we'll head home sometime after lunch."

"Sounds good. Are there going to be lots of people there?"

"Yeah, knowing my mom, probably."

Duncan snorted beside her. She shifted to look at him. "What?"

"Nothing," he muttered.

"Dunc isn't the biggest fan of my mom's gatherings."

"Why not?" Julia asked.

"Yeah, Dunc, why not?" Kasey's eyes gleamed with amusement when he glanced towards them. Oh no, what had she gotten herself in to?

"Let's just say Kasey's mom likes her parties to be memorable."

Julia wrinkled her nose. "What do you mean, memorable? What kind of parties does she like?"

Kasey laughed. "Nothing like you are worried about, darlin'. She likes party games and makes sure everyone is involved."

Duncan snorted. "Last time she had a freaking stage in the backyard with karaoke."

"Wow, did you sing?" Julia asked. She couldn't picture either man getting up and singing on the stage.

Duncan groaned, causing Kasey to burst out laughing. "My mom made Dunc sing a duet with her."

Julia covered her mouth as she laughed. "Oh my god, she did not."

"Unfortunately, she did. Kasey's 'shy'." Duncan air quoted. "So he got reprieve on the singing. Kasey told me I was a guest, so it'd be fine if I didn't sing. Barb had other plans." Duncan shook his head. "Jesus, it was awful."

"Well, come on, she had to get you up on stage, so all the ladies had a chance to see the goods," Kasey joked.

"What do you mean, all the ladies could see him?" Julia asked.

"My mom likes to round up all the single ladies she can find in her efforts to marry us all off, and the last few times she's been really focused on Duncan."

Duncan rubbed the back of his neck and groaned, causing Kasey to laugh again. "Last time she made Dunc sit through quite the lecture on how to treat a lady. She assumed he must be doing something wrong, otherwise some woman would have snatched him up by now."

"Oh lord," He grimaced. "I don't know how you got out of that conversation."

"I was given a reprieve because it would be 'weird' to talk about certain things with her son."

"She could have spared me the talk about not being a selfish lover, as no woman likes that, I was told." Duncan shuddered. "It was mortifying."

Julia chuckled. "Well, she's not wrong."

Duncan turned around in his seat and looked at Julia. "Can't say I've heard you complain," he said. He gave her a sizzling look before his gaze slowly traveled down her body and lingered on her breasts. He licked his lips as he stared at her, and Julia felt her nipples bead tightly against her bra.

"You okay, Jules?" Duncan asked, with a wicked smirk on his lips.

"Eyes front, cowboy," she told him.

"You sure? I could slide back there and take the edge off for you?" Duncan told her, which caused Kasey to growl.

"Not a chance. I'd drive us in to the fucking ditch if I could hear you two behind me and only catch glimpses in the rearview."

Kasey's gaze locked with hers in the rearview mirror. "But I'd be happy to pull over somewhere and help Duncan out." He winked. "I'm a team player, after all."

"No." She pointed at Kasey, then Duncan. "You both can stop that right now. We fucked all night long in preparation for this weekend of celibacy."

"I still don't know why I have to be celibate," Kasey muttered.

"Team player, man, team player," Duncan said, as he smacked Kasey on the arm. "If I can't fuck anyone this weekend, no one can. Solidarity."

"Exactly," Julia said. "So, you both need to knock off the heated looks and dirty comments."

Kasey's parents were expecting them by late afternoon and if she gave in and acted on the looks Duncan was sending her, they'd be late, and she'd look sex rumpled and that was not how she wanted to meet Kasey's family for the first time.

"I can't even talk dirty?" Kasey asked. "Jesus," he muttered.

"Nope, I told you if Duncan has to go without any fun, we all do," Julia reminded him.

"Told you I was her favorite," Duncan said, with a cheeky grin.

Kasey growled from the driver's seat. Duncan laughed and leaned over from the passenger seat, and dropped a quick kiss on Kasey's cheek. "It's a couple of days, dude. You've managed just fine in the past. Besides, who can get in the mood for anything sexy with all your mom's doilies and fake flowers and shit?"

Kasey laughed. "That's true. I banned her from putting that shit in my bedroom, otherwise I wouldn't have survived being a teenager."

Julia giggled at the idea of a teenaged Kasey trying to escape his mom's boner killing decorating. "It can't be that bad," she teased.

"Oh, just wait," Kasey told her.

"It's a good thing your mom's cooking makes up for her decorating skills," Duncan said. He turned in his seat, so he was facing her again. "His mom makes the best desserts you have ever seen. Prepare to need expanding pants by the end of the night." Duncan patted his flat stomach. "It's an orgy for the stomach. If I can't have sex at the Davison's, I can at least glutton myself on food."

"Please don't ever talk about my mom and orgy in the same sentence ever again," Kasey complained.

"What? Your mom is cute," Duncan teased. "That's where you get those great eyes from."

Kasey turned and glared at Duncan.

"It's true," Duncan told him.

"Mmm hmm," Kasey grumbled as he put his attention back on the road.

"I'm really looking forward to meeting everyone. This is going to be fun." Julia shifted in her seat and put her hand on Kasey's shoulder from the backseat and squeezed. He covered her hand with his before dropping his hand back down to the steering wheel.

"So, tell me about your sister. What's she like?" Julia asked.

"My sister is..." Kasey paused. "My sister is nothing like me."

"Well, that's not entirely true. She also got those fantastic eyes, and her mouth looks a lot like yours."

"Gross." Kasey scowled, then looked at Julia in the rearview mirror. "No, she's wild and loud and outgoing. She's always the life of the party. You'll like her, everyone does."

"I'm sure I will." Julia wrung her hands together. She was really nervous about this weekend. She hadn't grown up in a loving family. She didn't have any first-hand experience with what to expect other than what she'd seen on TV. The closest she'd seen was Kat, and her family was dysfunctional in its own way. What if Kasey's family didn't like her?

Duncan squeezed her knee, drawing her attention away from her thoughts. "Stop worrying, they're going to love you. Hell, they love me, so if I could win them over, it'll be a piece of cake for you to."

"Well, that's true." Julia laughed. It was going to be fine. She needed to just relax and be herself, and if they didn't like her, then, like Kasey had said, they only saw his family a couple of times a year, so who cares. And yet that sinking sensation in her stomach just wouldn't go away.

Chapter Eight

When they arrived at the house, Duncan took a deep, steadying breath. What had he been thinking, agreeing to come to this? He hated being here. Hated that Kasey was so ashamed of what was between them.

He grabbed his gear from the back of the truck and turned to see Kasey take Julia's hand in his. A sick feeling shot through him and settled in his gut. Was this the beginning of the end for them?

Before he'd taken more than a couple of steps, the front door whipped open, and Kasey's mom came barreling towards them with her arms outstretched.

It was hard to know by looking at her she was Kasey's mom. It seemed impossible to imagine someone as huge as Kasey coming out of such a tiny person. If she was even five feet tall, he'd eat his shirt. Her small size didn't stop her from pulling her son's face down for a smacking kiss before she turned and gave Julia the once over.

Julia shifted on her feet as if her nerves were getting the best of her.

Kasey's mom smiled and hugged Julia. "I'm so glad to meet you, Julia. My son's never brought anyone home to meet us before."

The simple statement cut deeper than Duncan could have imagined. He looked over and Kasey flashed him a look as if he was sorry. Well shit, if he was sorry, maybe he should just man up and tell his parents the truth.

Kasey's mom pulled away from Julia, then turned to Duncan. "Well, if it isn't the best-looking cowboy in the state. Get over here and give me a hug."

Duncan wrapped his arms around her. She always smelled the same. Kasey said it was lily of the valley or something like that. Whatever it was, every time he smelled it, he immediately thought of her.

"Nice to see you, Barb," Duncan said.

She pulled back and cupped his cheeks and rubbed the scruff on his face. "I like the beard."

"I thought you might. Just wanted you to know I listened to your advice the last time I was here." He winked at Barb and laughed when her face turned bright red.

"Oh you," she smacked him on the arm, then pulled him in for a tight hug. "Excellent decision," she whispered.

Duncan laughed, drawing everyone's attention back to them. Great, now he was the one with the red face.

Barb was always so warm and nice to him whenever he came. Hell, all of Kasey's family were. He didn't understand why Kasey was so scared to tell them the truth. They were a close-knit family. It didn't seem like anything would pull them apart. They were a whole lot closer than Duncan's family and his had been fine with him being bi-sexual. But then, maybe that was because they'd caught him messing around with his best friend when he was twelve. They had a little bit of a heads up on things, so when he'd finally admitted he liked both, it hadn't really come as a big surprise to his folks.

Kasey, on the other hand, had never even come close to being with another guy until Duncan.

"Duncan, I've put you in your normal room in the loft. We're a little short on beds with all the family coming in for the party, so you'll be packed in like sardines up there with the kids."

"He can bunk on the floor in my room, Mom, if you need the space," Kasey told her.

She rolled her eyes. "Don't be silly, Kasey. He can't bunk on the floor when you have your girlfriend in there."

Yeah, cuz that would be weird.

Kasey's eyes widened. "You put Julia in my room?"

"Oh course." She shook her head. "I realize I'm a bit old-fashioned at times, but I'm not completely naïve. You're young and healthy. I'm not going to kid myself that you aren't having sex." Barb hugged Kasey. "I'm just so happy you finally brought a woman home to meet us."

Jeez, could things get any worse? Not only was he relegated to the kiddy room, but Kasey and Julia were sleeping together, alone. Duncan rubbed the back of his neck, feeling the tension creeping across his shoulders.

He should have stayed home.
*****

The following morning, as Kasey filled his cup of coffee, he glanced out the window. Duncan was outside alone, sitting against the back fence, as far from the house as he could be.

Kasey filled a second cup and went outside. The door slammed shut behind him and Duncan's head snapped up. Even from across the yard, he could feel how pissed Duncan was.

Stopping in front of the other man, Kasey handed over the second cup of coffee.

"Have a good sleep?" The sarcasm in Duncan's voice matched the emotion swirling in his blue eyes.

"Yeah, you?"

"Just peachy." Duncan stared down at the ground, shutting Kasey out.

"Look, Dunc, I had no way of knowing my mom would let Julia sleep in my room."

"Nope."

"So, it's not like I planned it."

"Never said you did."

"Then why are you so pissy?"

Duncan's head whipped up. "Are you frickin' kidding me? You seriously don't know why I'm pissed?"

"Of course, I know why you're pissed, I just..." He shrugged. "It was out of my control."

"Actually, no it's not. If you'd man up and tell your parents about us, this wouldn't be an issue."

"There's a little more to it than manning up. My parents aren't like yours. They wouldn't understand."

"Right, cuz it's so easy for my family to understand. That's such crap and you know it. I'm not expecting your family to jump for joy but... Jesus, come on."

"Yeah, Jesus is kind of the point. My family is uber religious and you know it."

"And what? Don't they practice what they preach? Isn't the whole point to treat people how you'd like to be treated, judge not, and all that shit?"

"It's not that simple, Dunc."

"Maybe it is, and you don't give them enough credit."

Kasey raked his fingers through his hair. "No, I just don't see the point in upsetting them over something temporary."

Duncan's head snapped back. "Temporary?" he growled. "So that's all this is? We're just messing around until something better comes along?"

"No, that's not what I meant. But come on, you know I always saw myself married with kids and a wife."

"Right, and I kind of thought Julia fit the bill for both of us," Duncan said.

"Yeah, she does. She's perfect. That's kind of what I mean."

"Right, got it." Duncan threw the rest of his coffee on the lawn. "So, we're done?"

"No. Crap. That wasn't what I meant... I just... I don't know, Dunc. How do you see things playing out? It's not like we can both be with her long-term."

"Nope, guess not. Thanks for cluing me in." Duncan pushed his long, lean body off the ground and stormed off.

Yeah, that went well. The last thing Kasey wanted was to stop being with Duncan. He loved him more than anything. But being with a guy wasn't how he envisioned his life. Julia fit. She made sense. She was the easy choice.

Fuck. Coming home always messed with his head. Being back here with Julia. Listening to his mom talk, the way she described their future, he could imagine it. It would sure as hell be a lot simpler.

The problem was Julia fit with both of them. The three of them were what really worked. It was hard to imagine being with her without Duncan.

Duncan was right. He was a chickenshit. What he really wanted was to be with both of them long term. Honestly, as much as he hated to admit it, before Julia, he never thought he'd meet anyone that even came close to making him feel what Duncan did. He'd almost been ready to admit to his parents that he loved Dunc. But she had come along, and she made him feel things too. Being with Julia would just be easier. It wouldn't rock the boat, no one would have to accept an unconventional relationship. He could have the traditional life he was raised to want.

He looked towards the house where Duncan had gone. If being with Julia was right, then why did the idea of not being with Duncan make him feel so sick?

The three of them needed to sit down and figure things out. Unfortunately, knowing Duncan, that wouldn't be easy.

Especially when he was clearly hurt by how this weekend played out.

*****

So far, he'd managed to avoid any kind of conversation with Julia or Kasey. He looked across the pool to where they sat together on a big lounge chair. The perfect couple.

He'd just grabbed a beer out of the cooler and twisted off the cap when Lisa walked up to him.

"I'm really glad you came with my brother this weekend. Thanks for being here, Dunc."

"No problem, darlin'. You know I wouldn't miss your graduation for anything."

She stepped closer to him. "So, am I grown up enough for you now?"

Shit. "What do you mean?"

"I seem to remember us having a conversation a few years ago where I told you I loved you, and you said I was too young."

Duncan laughed. Man, she'd been drunk that night. "And you were. Hell, you were still in high school."

She trailed her finger down his bare stomach. "I know. But I'm a college graduate now. I'm all grown up, Dunc." She licked her lips in a practiced move.

Damn, she wasn't kidding. He scanned her body in her skimpy bathing suit. She looked good and if she wasn't Kasey's sister, and things were different with Jules, he might seriously consider giving her what she was asking for.

He glanced over at Kasey and Julia again. Who was he kidding? He was the odd man out in that combo now, and he knew it.

He brought his beer up to his mouth and poured as much as he could down his throat. Part of him had always known Kasey wasn't in it for the long haul, but after four years together, he just assumed things would stay as they were. Women would come and go, but at the end of the day, they'd still be together. Julia changed all that. Unfortunately, he'd been stupid enough to think that meant the three of them would be together, not that he'd be out.

Lisa ran her finger down the ridges in his abs, making him want to go grab a shirt and cover up. It felt wrong to have her flirting with him. He grabbed her wrist to stop the movement. "Look, Lise, you're a gorgeous woman and any guy would be lucky to have you but..." he paused.

"But you're in love with my brother," she finished.

"What?"

She cocked her head to the side and smiled. "I'm not an idiot, Dunc, despite what you and my brother think."

"What?" This couldn't be happening. How could Lisa know he was in love with Kasey?

"It's okay. I mean, sure, I'm disappointed that you aren't attracted to me, but it's nice to know that if I can't have you, at least you'll be with someone good."

"Yeah, your brother and I aren't together." He pointed towards Kasey and Julia. "As you can see."

Lisa's forehead wrinkled. "I thought you guys' shared lots of women."

Holy shit, he could not be having this conversation. He coughed. "Umm..."

"Oh, come on, Duncan. I'm not a baby. I've heard all the stories about you two. Hell, I know girls you've been with."

"Okay, so then you know we aren't together during those threesomes."

She looked over at Julia and Kasey and back at him. From the look in her eyes, he could see the wheels firing. "Not usually, no. But I think things are different with her."

"Oh yeah, why's that, smart girl?"

Lisa shrugged. "I don't know. Something about the way you all look at each other."

"Well, you're wrong. Your brother's a traditionalist. He's a wife and two-point-four kids' kind of guy."

"My brother's an idiot."

Duncan wrapped his arms around Lisa and pulled her into a hug. He couldn't argue with that. "Your brother underestimates you, darlin'"

"He always has." Lisa stepped back and smiled. Her eyes sparkled with mischief. "So, what do you say we give him something to think about?"

He glanced over his shoulder and saw Kasey watching them from across the deck. "What'd you have in mind?"

"Well, if I know my brother, jealousy is an amazing motivator."

"Jealousy?"

"Mmm hmm."

Duncan released a deep breath. "What'd you have in mind?"

"Who's up for chicken fights?" Lisa yelled to the group as she grabbed Duncan's hand and dragged him towards the pool.

"Jesus," he muttered. This wasn't going to end well.

Chapter Nine

Over breakfast the next morning, Duncan watched the interaction between Kasey and Julia. They seemed closer this weekend than they previously had, more intimate. Kasey's hand dipped below the table and his arm angled towards Julia like he had his hand on her knee. Julia smiled at Kasey. She glanced at Duncan and gave him a tight smile, almost like she felt guilty. But why? Sure, Kasey and Julia had slept in the same room, and he'd be an idiot to think they hadn't fucked, despite their agreement, but what did she have to feel guilty about? His mind raced as he imagined all the possible scenarios.

What if they'd realized that they were better off without him in their relationship? It sure as hell would be easier for them.

Fuck, he needed some time to think and figure all this shit out.

"I'm going to get a ride back home with Lisa," Duncan announced to the table.

"Excuse me?" Kasey said as he sat up straight from the table. He pinned Duncan with an angry glare.

"I'm going to get a ride home with Lisa. Well, actually she's going to let me drive her hot new car," Duncan said, and winked at Lisa.

"Our place is totally out of her way. It doesn't make sense for her to drive you," Kasey replied.

"Finally," Kasey's mom said. "I've been waiting forever for you two to make eyes at each other." The older woman smiled gleefully. "I knew if I put you together often enough, something would happen."

Duncan coughed. "Um, yeah, no, Barb, it's not like that."

Lisa laughed and patted Duncan on the arm. "No, Mother, Duncan has not suddenly fallen in love with me. I have some stuff I need moved and Dunc graciously agreed to help me," Lisa piped in.

"Whatever you say, dear," their mom chirped.

Lisa pushed off from the table. "And on that note, we should probably head out pretty quick, Dunc, so I don't keep you all night. We both have to work tomorrow, and I promised I'd feed you if you helped me."

"You aren't coming to church?" Barb asked.

"Nope, sorry we can't if we are going to get everything done today," Lisa said.

Duncan stood up and Kasey pushed up from the table. "We need to talk," Kasey growled.

Once they were in the hallway, Duncan spoke. "What's there to talk about?"

Kasey shook his head and continued down the hall away from the dining room and towards the bedrooms.

Once they were away from prying ears, Duncan grabbed Kasey's arm. "You wanted to talk, so are you planning on talking to me?"

"What the fuck is going on with you and my sister?"

"Oh, come on man, I'm not going to fucking touch your sister and you know it." Duncan snarled.

"Well, what the hell have you been doing sniffing around her all weekend? And now you're getting a ride home with her?" Kasey snapped.

"What did you want me to do, Kase? Huh, sit around and cry into my beer in the corner while you snuggled up with Julia so that no one in your family or this shitty little town thinks you're gay."

"I'm not gay," Kasey growled.

"Well, you sure fuck like you are," Duncan said.

Kasey pushed Duncan in the chest and his back hit the wall. "You're an asshole," Kasey snarled.

"And you're a fucking coward." He'd had enough of this shit. He pushed away from the wall.

"Why are you getting a ride home with my sister?"

Duncan angrily pushed his fingers through his hair. Guess they were doing this now. "Because I need some time to think, and I can't do that in the car with you and Jules."

"What do you need to think about?" Kasey asked.

Duncan wrapped his hand around the back of Kasey's neck and pulled his head towards him for a hard, punishing kiss. Kasey broke the kiss and shoved Duncan in the chest, and glanced nervously down the hall.

"Yeah, that's what I thought," Duncan muttered. "Don't worry, no one is around to see anything."

"What the fuck are you doing? You know how it needs to be here," Kasey pitched his voice low. "I know this sucks, but now is not the time to discuss it."

"When is it ever?" Duncan grumbled. Overwhelming sadness swept through him as he looked at Kasey's panic strickened face. "Come on, Kase, they love you. They wouldn't fucking care."

"It's not your decision to make," Kasey snarled.

"Jesus, you are so far in the closet. It's like we live in fucking Narnia and your parents' place is the real world for you." Duncan took a step back and rubbed his face roughly with his hands. "I'm such an idiot. This was never going to be real for you."

"Dunc," Kasey said. "Come on, let's not do this now."

"No, you're right. We don't need to do this now. I've been in love with you since the day we met and you've never..." He sighed. What was the point?

Kasey glanced over his shoulder, stiffened, then relaxed. Duncan looked behind him and saw Julia standing in the hallway.

Duncan straightened. "I'm going to get a ride home with Lisa, and then I'll stay in one of the staff cabins tonight until we figure something else out."

Julia stepped forward and put her hand on Duncan's arm. "What do you mean, stay in the staff cabin? Why wouldn't you sleep at home?"

Duncan glanced at Kasey. He looked pissed. Now was not the time to get into this. Kasey's jaw clenched tight as he stared at Duncan.

Duncan wrapped his arms around Julia and squeezed her tightly. He inhaled, memorizing the scent of her shampoo.

"Talk to me, Duncan," she urged.

He shuddered. He didn't want to let her go. How did everything get so fucked up, when just a few days ago he'd been the happiest he'd ever been?

"Look after him, Jules," he whispered and kissed her forehead.

He turned on his heel and walked towards the bedroom to grab his bag. Who was he kidding? Kasey would never want what he wanted. He was a traditionalist, Duncan wasn't. He'd always been the kind of guy who said fuck societal norms. He'd been chasing what felt good his entire life and look where it had gotten him. The man and woman he was in love with were with each other, and he was out on his own. He needed to get the hell out of here. His eyes burned as he fought back the tears that threatened to fall.

*****

Duncan's phone buzzed in his pocket for the third time. He pushed his half-empty beer further onto the bar. Changing the angle of his hips, he shifted on the seat so he could reach the phone. Kasey's number flashed on the caller id.

Man, he was a pussy. Just seeing Kasey's name made his heart race. He couldn't deny that a huge part of him hoped that the other man was calling to suck up. To admit that he'd made a mistake.

Duncan punched the button to listen to his voicemail, and Kasey's worried voice came across the line.

"I'm not kidding around, Dunc. If you know where she is, call me."

What the hell was he talking about? If he knew where who was?

Damn, why did his voicemail have to play the most recent message first?

He quickly deleted the message so he could get to the first message left. His stomach sank when he heard Kasey's pained message about how Julia had taken off because she didn't want to come between them.

Shit, they had to find her.

He threw a ten-dollar bill on the bar and grabbed his jacket off the back of the chair. Turns out the fact that he'd pathetically been nursing the same beer for the past hour and a half was a good thing. He could still drive.

Racing across the parking lot with his keys in one hand, he quickly dialed Kasey back with the other.

"Where the hell have you been?" Kasey demanded.

"I'm on my way." Duncan pulled open the door of the truck and climbed in.

"We fucked up, man."

"Story of my life," Duncan murmured. "But what do you mean, she's gone?"

"This afternoon she said she wanted to give me some space to think, so she was going to go out for a bit. But she never came home. Now she's not returning my calls and when I went into the bedroom a few minutes ago, I found a note she'd left on the bed that she was leaving because she didn't want to come between us," Kasey told him.

"Shit," Duncan muttered. "Where are you now?"

"I'm just driving around aimlessly. I don't have a clue where to look."

"Did you talk to Kat?" Duncan switched his phone to his other hand and fired up the truck.

"Yeah, I called her. She hasn't seen her."

"She hasn't seen her, or she hasn't talked to her?" Frustrated, Duncan rubbed the back of his neck.

"What's the difference?" Kasey asked.

"This is Kat we're talking about. Semantics are everything. She doesn't like to lie, but there's a lot of gray area for her." He needed to see her in person and they'd better get answers out of Kat, otherwise he didn't have the first clue where to look for her.

"Fuck, I don't remember what she said exactly," Kasey muttered.

"I'll meet you at their place. Kat has a terrible poker face. She sucks at playing the word games face to face."

"K, I'll see you there. Hurry, man."

Duncan dialed Julia's number. He slammed his hands on the steering wheel when his call went directly to voicemail. *Fuck.*

He tossed his phone on the passenger seat, threw the truck into drive, and squealed out of the bar parking lot. His phone beeped from the seat beside him, alerting him to a text message. Lunging, he grabbed the phone and saw a text from Lisa.

Julia is fine. She's at my place.

What the fuck?

Why was Julia at Kasey's sister's place? Guess he'd be finding out soon enough. He quickly dialed Kasey.

"Change of plans. Meet me at your sister's," Duncan said, as soon as Kasey answered the phone.

"Why would I meet you at Lisa's?"

"Because that's where Julia is." Duncan's mind raced as he tried to process why Julia might be at Lisa's. Of all the places she could go, why there?

"Why the hell would she be at my sister's?" Kasey growled.

"I don't know, but Lisa just texted me that she's there."

"Why would my sister have texted you?"

Jesus. Were they really going to get into this kind of shit when they could be looking for Julia? "I don't know. Why don't we ask her when we get there?"

Kasey was silent for several seconds before he finally exhaled loudly. "On my way."

Minutes later, Duncan slammed the brakes in front of Lisa's house. He threw the car in park and ran towards Kasey at the bottom of the stairs. "Did you talk to her?" he asked.

"No, I waited for you." Kasey's stare trailed across Duncan's face. "You look like shit, man."

"Gee thanks, I wonder why."

"I'm sorry, Dunc." Those expressive eyes that Duncan had always loved were filled with sadness.

"I know, me too. We'll figure out our shit after we talk to Julia and make sure she's okay." Unfortunately for both of them, he already knew how this conversation was going to go.

Kasey sighed. "Maybe that's the problem. Maybe we need to figure out our shit first, so Julia knows where she stands."

"What do you mean?" Duncan asked. "How does she not know where she stands? It's pretty clear you want to be with her."

"Well, obviously I do." Kasey tucked his hands into the pockets of his jeans and looked down at his boots. "But so do you."

Duncan shrugged. "What I want doesn't seem to matter too much here."

"What do you mean? Of course, it matters." Kasey's forehead wrinkled as he looked at him.

"Clearly it doesn't, Kase. What I want is a relationship with both of you. Like we talked about. Like we've been doing for the past couple of months. I thought what we had was pretty fucking great."

"It was," Kasey replied. "It's just not realistic."

"Why not?" Duncan asked. "Because you aren't gay? FYI Kasey, we fuck, you're not straight." He shook his head. "Who the hell cares about some label that some asshole wants to give you?"

"It's not about labels," Kasey grumbled.

"Oh yeah? Then what's it about?" Duncan demanded. "Because you aren't going to find anything better than what we had, what the three of us had." Duncan stepped closer to Kasey. "No one can make you feel what we can."

Kasey's eyes darkened, and Duncan could see his pulse beating hard in his neck.

Duncan smirked. Kasey might kid himself, but the lust between them wasn't going anywhere. "You still want me."

"I never said I didn't," Kasey replied.

"You just don't want to."

"Honestly, no, I don't. It would be a fuck-ton easier if I didn't want you," Kasey growled. "How do you see this working out long term, Dunc? Huh?" Kasey yelled. "It's not like we can just live as a threesome forever."

"Why not?" Duncan asked.

"What do you mean, why not? Because people don't do that. They grow up. They have families. They can't keep being ruled by their dicks for the rest of their lives."

"Is that what this is between us? It's just your dick? That's it?" Duncan stepped towards him, so they were chest to chest. Kasey closed his eyes.

"You know it's not," Kasey whispered. He opened his eyes and the pain in them nearly brought Duncan to his knees.

It killed him to see Kasey struggling like this, but he had to decide for himself what mattered. Duncan couldn't make this decision for him, and he wasn't willing to keep living the lie. It hurt too much to be Kasey's dirty little secret.

"What do you want from me, Dunc?" Kasey asked. His voice cracked with pain.

"Honestly? I want to be yours. Openly. Publicly." He sighed. "Before Julia, I didn't really care. I knew you were in the closet with your family and that was fine. I probably could have gone on like that forever. But seeing you with Jules and your family, seeing you being so open and affectionate with her in front of them? It killed me. Not because I was jealous of her, exactly, but because I was jealous that you would never be like that with me. I was this outsider, watching the people I love be happy in a way I'd never get to be." His throat burned as he tried to quell the emotion. "Fuck, I sound like such a girl." He sniffed.

"It's not like I wanted to exclude you." Kasey's shoulders slumped. He looked down at his feet, then raised his pained stare back to Duncan's.

"But that's the thing, Kase, you are choosing to exclude me. You could be open with your parents about us. But you don't want to tell them. It's a choice. And that choice fucking sucks for me." Duncan stepped back from Kasey. "I deserve better than that. I deserve to be with someone who isn't ashamed of me."

"I'm not ashamed of you," Kasey told him.

Duncan stared at the man he loved, his heart breaking for Kasey. "No, you're ashamed of yourself, and that's the real problem."

Kasey sucked in a breath. They stared at each other for several moments. When Kasey didn't say anything, Duncan sighed. *Guess that was his answer.*

"As much as I love Julia, what I want is the three of us." Duncan rubbed his face. The sound of his hand scratching against his whiskers echoed through the quiet night air. Why did this have to be so hard? "You guys were really happy together this weekend. You clearly love her, and she can give you everything you've ever wanted. The wife, the kids, the perfect family." Duncan sighed. "I love you, Kasey, and what kind of asshole would I be if I stood in the way of that dream?"

"What kind of asshole would I be if I stopped you from being with the woman you loved?" Kasey asked him.

"It's not the same and you know it." Sadness filled his chest at what could have been if Kasey was just brave enough to try.

Duncan squared his shoulders. "Let's go talk to Julia."

Kasey stared at him. He opened his mouth to speak, then closed it. He sighed. "This fucking sucks."

"Yep."

"Are you idiots done deciding my life for me?" Julia called from the side of the house.

Chapter Ten

"Jules?" Kasey called.

Julia came around the side of the house. She glanced back and forth between the two, sadness pulled at the corners of her green eyes, making her look tired and alone. It took everything in Kasey not to pull her into his arms.

"What are you doing here?" Duncan asked.

"Kat was out this afternoon, and I didn't know where to go or who to talk to and was just kind of rambling around this afternoon when Lisa called and asked me to come over to talk."

Kasey looked at Duncan. "Did you talk to my sister about us?"

"Your sister has known about us for years."

What the actual fuck? Kasey's stomach knotted as a wave of nausea swept through him. "What do you mean my sister knows?" Kasey asked.

Duncan shrugged. "I mean, she's known for a long time."

Julia nodded. "That's what she told me, too."

"Well shit," Kasey muttered.

Julia stepped towards him. "Your sister doesn't care that we are all in a relationship together. If anything, she thought it was pretty awesome."

Why wouldn't she have said something to him if she knew?

Kasey shook his head. "I can't even wrap my head around this. How the hell did she know?"

"She said Duncan made you happy in a way she'd never seen before, so she started really paying attention to you two over the years." Julia placed her hand on his chest. "The only other person she has seen you this happy with is me."

And look where that got him. "But you left," Kasey muttered.

"I can't be the person who comes between you two. I love you both so much. How can I be the cause of your relationship falling apart?"

If only it were that simple. This thing between Duncan and him blowing up had been years in the making. "You aren't the reason it fell apart, Jules."

"I know that, now, after talking to your sister and then hearing you two fight."

She looked at Duncan and gave his hand a quick squeeze before turning back to Kasey.

"You don't get to decide what's right for me. Either of you." Julia straightened her spine. "When I came here a few months ago, I felt broken, empty." She sniffed. "No, more than that. I felt worthless."

Kasey groaned. It gutted him to hear her talk like that.

"Jules," Duncan said, taking her hand.

"No, let me finish," she argued. "You changed that for me. Both of you." She looked them both in the eyes. "Being with you, loving you, being loved by you both made me feel valued and worthy in a way I've never known before." She wiped the tears that ran down her cheeks as she spoke. "I'm with Duncan on this one. I don't want this to end. I'm in love with you both. It wouldn't feel right to be with either of you without the other. We fit, the three of us."

Kasey groaned. "But how would that work long term, Jules? People will talk. It's different being here in our bubble." He looked at Duncan. "Like you said Dunc, it's Narnia."

Duncan rubbed his chest. His eyes glistened with moisture as he stared back at Kasey. The confidence he normally saw in Duncan's cocky stance no longer visible as his shoulders slumped.

Julia leaned into Duncan and whispered something quietly to him. She linked their arms and pulled him, so they were both standing in front of Kasey.

"What if it doesn't have to be one or the other? What if you can have it all? Did you ever think of that? This right here." She swept her arm out towards the city.

"What we have is as real as it gets. The way I feel when I'm with you both. The way I know Duncan feels about both of us. That's real Kasey." She pulled Duncan a step closer to him so they were both almost touching him. "People loving you, just you, for who you are, wanting to put your needs first and protect you. That's rare, Kase. It doesn't come along very often, trust me."

She pushed her body up against him, drawing Duncan along his other side. "What we have is special. It's a gift. Your sister told me she fully approves of us all and she thinks your parents will too once they get used to the idea. She said they just want you to be happy. They love Duncan and already think of him as part of the family." Julia wrapped her arms around Kasey's waist.

She leaned her weight against him, and Duncan's body pressed up against his side. He shuddered. He wanted this as badly as they did. But fuck, it scared him. How could this possibly work?

"It's not realistic," Kasey whispered.

"Neither is truly falling in love with two people, but we seem to all have done that," Julia replied. "Unless you don't actually love Duncan and I."

"You know I do," he groaned. "Love isn't the problem."

Julia nudged Duncan's arm, and he curled his hand around the back of Kasey's neck. Kasey turned his head and leaned his cheek against Duncan's palm. God, he wanted to believe them. Beneath the pain in Duncan's eyes, Kasey swore he saw a glimmer of hope that Julia was right, and they could make this work.

"Don't you think what we have is worth fighting for, Kase?" Duncan asked.

"Of course it is. I just don't want to prolong the inevitable."

"It's only inevitable if we decide it is," Julia said.

God, she was so naïve. That wasn't how society worked. He truly would love to believe it was just that simple, but he knew otherwise. "I don't know, Jules, you both seem to have this romanticized view of the world."

Julia snorted. "Yeah, growing up in a house that was constantly filled with domestic violence was a dream come true."

"That's not what I meant," Kasey muttered.

"No, I know that. But what I'm saying is, my mom worked really hard to mold herself to be the perfect little wife, the perfect little girlfriend, to fit that stereotypical picture. But at what cost?" Julia shook her head. "She sure as hell wasn't happy. I wasn't happy, so what was the point of it all?" She leaned back and looked at Kasey. "Was that life better for any of us than what we could provide for each other just because it fit that picture that society says it should?" She angrily wiped a tear from her face. "I'd rather have what we have and deal with the talk than what I grew up with any day of the week."

"You say that now, but how would you have felt if you had been a kid with two dads and a mom? All the talk. People saying your mom's a slut." Kasey pushed away from them.

"We are a long way from having kids, Kase," Duncan told him.

"I know that, but I want kids at some point, so it's something we have to factor into this decision." He'd always pictured himself as a father and that wasn't a dream he was willing to give up. And he saw that life as a real possibility with Julia. He just couldn't reconcile how to have that with Duncan too, despite how much it gutted him to think about a life without him beside him. "People can be really cruel, and I'm not going to have them talk about you that way, Jules, or make my kid feel ashamed or ostracized. It's not fair to any child I might have."

"You know what wasn't fair, Kasey? Having my mom not be able to come to my school concerts because she was laid up in bed after her most recent boyfriend used her as a punching bag. Not being able to afford a prom dress because my mom gave the boyfriend de jour my savings to pay for his debts." Julia paced away from them. "Or maybe it was the final straw of my mom trying to force me to fuck her boyfriend because it would make him 'really happy' and then kicking me out when I wouldn't." She angrily swiped her arm across her face to wipe the tears that streamed down her cheeks.

My god, hearing her speak about her childhood was crushing. He had no idea it had been that bad for her. She was stronger than he'd ever imagined. With her history, it was even more amazing that she felt confident enough to stand up to them. Kasey clenched his hands tightly together to stop himself from reaching for her, from trying to take her pain away. She had fought so hard to be strong enough to stand on her own, and he would not take that from her.

"I would have fucking been over the moon to have one parent who truly loved me and put me first. We can offer a child three. Three fucking people that would die for them. Do you know how lucky that kid would be?" Julia yelled.

"So, fucking lucky," Duncan murmured. Julia's head whipped around, and she looked at Duncan.

Duncan reached up and tucked her hair behind her ear and stared down at her. "You're right, any kid that might result from this relationship would be fine. They'd have three parents willing to go to the mat for them, and who couldn't use an extra person in their corner?

Julia smiled, then they both turned to Kasey.

"Jesus." Kasey exhaled. "You make it sound like it could all be so easy."

"It's not easy, Kase. Life is fucking hard," Duncan snapped. "But it's a whole lot better when you have people you love fighting with you."

Duncan clasped Julia's hand and pulled her up against him. "I'm with Jules. I think what we have is worth any fight."

Julia's beautiful face softened as she smiled at him. "We can figure this out together, Kasey."

His heart thumped in his chest as he looked at the two people he loved. In a perfect world he'd be all in, but this world was so fucking far from perfect. Did he dare risk it?

Hand-in-hand, they stepped towards Kasey. "Yeah, it could be weird, but it's a whole new world, and you two are confident and cocky enough to get anyone on your side."

"I don't know if that's true, but Dunc definitely has the cocky down pat," Kasey joked.

"It's not cocky if you have the goods to back it up." Duncan winked. "Come on, Kase, we can make this work. Trust us."

Kasey sighed. What should he do? He raised his head up to the sky and prayed. He could feel Julia and Duncan watching him closely as he silently asked for answers.

He took a deep breath and opened his eyes to find them both waiting expectantly.

"My sister was really okay with everything?"

"More than okay." Julia nodded.

"I don't know." Kasey silently looked up at the sky for several moments, then finally spoke. "Everything I've been raised to believe says that I shouldn't want this. That it's wrong and I don't..." he sighed.

The front door opened, and Lisa walked out. "Sorry to interrupt, I know this is private, but I could hear you inside, and Kase, you're a fucking idiot," Lisa told him as she came down the stairs.

"Wha... what do you mean?" he stammered.

"Mom and Dad raised us in the church, but they also raised us to trust our hearts and our guts, and that God would always have our back. So, if they can't get on board with you finding love with Duncan and Julia, then they are hypocrites, and there's no way I'm going to tolerate that." She squared her shoulders and stared Kasey down. "Believe me, by the time I'm done with them, they will have accepted it."

Duncan wrapped his arm around Lisa and grinned. "Baby sister is all grown up," he cheered.

"No shit," Kasey muttered. "You're really okay with all this?"

"I love you, Kase, and I'm always going to have your back. You know that. Mom and Dad will support you too. It just might take them a bit, and they might have to find a new church family." She wrinkled her nose and chuckled.

"Fuck," Kasey groaned.

"Not your problem, big brother. You gotta do you."

"Your parents are amazing. Even if they don't like it at first, Lisa's right, they will come around. They love you, Kasey. I've seen it," Duncan told him.

God, he wanted to believe they could make this work because the alternative of not being with them was unbearable. Kasey took a deep breath and rolled his neck. "Yeah, maybe you're right. Time for them to put their money where their mouth is with all this church stuff. Judge not, right?"

Lisa walked over to Kasey and pulled him into a hug. "Don't fuck up the best thing that's ever happened to you, Kase. You're an adult. You get to choose your life," she whispered.

The knot that had been in his chest this entire weekend eased at the love and support from his sister. She was right. He'd be a fucking idiot not to see where this thing went with Julia and Duncan.

He turned back around and held Duncan's stare for several seconds, then looked at Julia. "Fuck, I love you both," Kasey groaned.

Julia squealed and wrapped her arms around Kasey's neck and planted a loud smacking kiss against his lips, making both Duncan and Kasey laugh.

Duncan pushed his way into their hug. He cupped the back of Kasey's neck and brought their mouths together for a soft kiss. Kasey jolted at the pressure, as it was so much different from the heated kisses Duncan normally gave him. This wasn't a lustful kiss, but a sweet, loving kiss of connection.

Duncan wrapped his arm around Kasey and his left around Julia, and pulled them both against the sides of his body. "Let's go home," he told them.

"Call me later," Lisa yelled.

"He's not getting near a phone tonight, Lise," Duncan called back.

"Gross," Lisa laughed.

Julia smacked him on the chest. "Duncan," she scolded.

"What? It's true." Duncan raised his eyebrows and looked at Julia, then at Kasey. Kasey licked his lips and Duncan's eyes darkened as they looked at each other.

"I'll call you tomorrow, Lise." Kasey pulled Duncan and Julia towards their vehicles.

"I'll meet you at home. Drive fast," Duncan hollered as he jogged to his truck.

Kasey slid behind the steering wheel of the truck, and Julia jumped into the passenger seat beside him. He smiled to himself as he turned the key in the ignition.

Things were a long way from perfect, but together they'd figure it out. He turned to Julia and grabbed her hand. "Let's go home."

Epilogue

One year later

She leaned back in the chair. Her eyes lingered on a large drawing of a skull with snakes and bugs crawling all over it. It was definitely not her thing, but there was no denying the artist who had created it was amazing.

Duncan reached over and grabbed her hand. "You ready to do this?"

She squeezed his fingers, then wove her right hand with Kasey's. "Absolutely." She exhaled. "Who's going first?"

She looked at the two men expectantly and laughed when neither of them spoke. What a couple of babies. They thought nothing of leaping off a horse onto the back of a running calf, but a little tattoo was enough to make them both shudder.

"I'll go first, but don't you dare chicken out on me." She pinned them both with her fiercest glare.

"Don't worry, darlin', we won't chicken out." Duncan picked up her left hand and placed a kiss against her knuckles.

Kasey nudged her leg. "Looks like we're up," he said and tilted his head towards the back of the tattoo parlor.

Julia looked up and watched the artist as he walked towards them. Justice Saunders had a reputation as one of the best artists in the state.

A few months back, Kat had written an article on him and they'd quickly become friends, which is how they ended up here today. He'd painted such a tempting picture about the power of tattoos and the symbolism and meaning they could portray.

She'd been sold. It had taken a little convincing to get the men on board, but she'd worn them down.

"Okay guys, I'm ready for you all to come back," Justice said. "The shop doesn't open for a couple hours, so there's lots of room for you all to come back together all at once."

They all pushed off from their chairs and followed Justice to his station.

"So Jules, I'm confident what I drew up for Kasey and Duncan will work perfectly but I'm not 100% sure yours will fit exactly, so I may need to tweak a couple of things on yours," Justice said as he looked at the small stencil in his hand.

"What do you mean, why wouldn't mine work?" she asked.

Kasey took her hand in his and kissed her knuckles. *Weird.* Duncan had just done the exact same thing. "What's going on?" she asked

"I know we can't do the normal marriage thing," Kasey said.

"Right, that's why we are getting matching tattoos," she replied. She looked between her two men. What was going on? They both looked so nervous. Certainly more nervous than was necessary over a little matching tattoo they were all getting on their hips. Her stomach flipped at the intensity of the way they were both watching her. What were they up to?

"Exactly, but Duncan and I got talking about how not only are you missing out on the whole marriage, but you are also missing out on the engagement and wedding rings and everything that publicly shows the world you are taken." Kasey's thumb rubbed against her ring finger.

"Ok?" she replied. Her heart pounded in her chest. Where was he going with this?

Duncan and Kasey both dropped to their knees in front of her. Holy shit, was this really happening right now? She covered her mouth with her hands. Oh my god, oh my god, oh my god. She flicked a glance at Justice standing beside her, and he winked.

"Jules, I know this life we've all chosen is unconventional," Kasey said.

"That's putting it mildly," Duncan snorted.

Kasey scowled at him. "Seriously?"

"Sorry, continue." Duncan hung his head like a chastised child, causing Julia to laugh. Even when they were making a grand romantic gesture, Duncan couldn't help joking around, and Kasey had no time for his shenanigans but the love between them was evident by the way they were leaning against each other, united as they looked up at her.

"I know we all agreed we are in this for life. That we are all committed and nothing will change that," Kasey said. "In our minds, we are all already married."

"So with us working on the ranch and you now working back in a restaurant kitchen, a ring is tricky," Duncan said.

"Right." Julia smiled down at them both as they kneeled before her so calmly on the floor of the tattoo parlor. God, she loved these men.

"So we asked Justice if he could make us matching wedding ring tattoos instead," Duncan said.

"That way, even though we can't legally get married, we still can have something that tells us and the world that we are together. A symbol of commitment," Kasey told her.

"Oh my god, you guys," Julia whispered. Tears burned behind her eyes as the gravity of what they were offering set in. "Are you serious that you want to do this?" she asked. "Kase? Yeah?"

Kasey stood up and wrapped his arms around her and pulled her tightly against him. "Nothing would make me prouder than letting the world know you are mine." He reached down and pulled Duncan up and into their hug. "Both of you."

Tears ran down Julia's cheeks as she hugged her guys. They had come such a long way in the past year. There had been a few bumps along the way, some of them pretty freaking huge, but they'd weathered them all. And Duncan was right, having someone else fighting the fights with you made it bearable.

"So we doing this?" Justice asked.

"Absolutely," Julia replied. She pressed a kiss to Kasey's lips, then Duncan's, before turning back to Justice. "Let's get committed."

Kasey groaned. "God, that sounds awful."

Julia laughed. "Well, a girl would have to be crazy to link herself to you two for a lifetime." She sat down on the tattoo table and looked up at her guys. "Seriously you two, thank you. I love this idea. Every day I feel so blessed to be with you both, and I want the entire world to know you're mine."

She held out her hand for Justice to put the stencil on her finger. "Let's put a ring on it," she said and wiggled her hand.

"You are such a goofball," Duncan laughed.

"You love it," she said as she blinked up and him and batted her eyes.

"You're right I do." He kissed her, then cupped the back of Kasey's neck. "She said yes," he told him.

"She said yes," Kasey replied and pressed a kiss against Duncan's lips.

"Was there ever any doubt?" Julia asked.

"No, not really. I mean, we'd already had the talk, but tattooing a ring on your finger is a different level of commitment," Duncan said.

"No more so than a tattoo on my hip. This one just means a lot more now." She loved the idea of a permanent reminder of their commitment and a ring that she could see every time she looked down was even better than what they had originally planned. This symbol told everyone they belonged to each other. A year ago, she never would have imagined they'd be here. How did she get so lucky?

Justice adjusted the stencil and pulled it off, then brought out a marker and began drawing on her finger. Several minutes later, he stepped back and nodded. "Alright, what do you think?"

Julia looked down at her finger and the intricate, knotted design that Justice had drawn. She brought her hand up closer to inspect it. "Is that our initials woven in there?" she asked.

"Yeah. The guys gave me free rein on the design. They just said you liked Celtic designs and asked for me to stay within that theme and weaving your initials in felt like a fun addition. You have to look closely to figure out that's how they are linked together, but I thought it worked," Justice said.

Tears welled in her eyes again. "Oh my god, Justice. It more than works. This is going to be gorgeous."

"Alright, then, let's get you inked." He sat down on his stool, and Kasey and Duncan pulled up their chairs on the other side of the table. Kasey took her hand in his and placed it on her thigh and Duncan's fingers linked with theirs as all their hands rested on her leg in an intertwined pile.

It felt like no time at all before Justice was done with all three tattoos. Justice took several photos of the rings with their hands placed in various artistic positions. "I'll email these to you," he told them.

"That would be amazing." Julia looked down at her hand. Warmth spread through her chest and a huge smile broke out across her face. This must be what women felt like when they looked down at their engagement rings. She wiggled her fingers. She couldn't wait to show this off to everyone.

"We are stopping at Kat's on the way home to show her."

Kasey laughed. His eyes sparkled with love as he smiled at her indulgently. "I wouldn't have expected anything less."

They walked towards the front of the shop and stopped at the front counter to pay.

"Don't worry about it, it's on me," Justice told them.

"What? No. We agreed on the price when we talked about the design change," Duncan said.

"Yeah, well, that was before I got to be a part of this whole love fest." Justice rolled his eyes. "Let's just call it a wedding present."

Julia wrapped her arms around his broad frame. "Thank you," she said and placed a kiss against his bearded cheek. "I couldn't have asked for a better gift from anyone."

"My pleasure, Jules. Wear it with pride. You guys are lucky to have found what you have. Don't let anyone tell you otherwise." Justice's gruff face stared down at her.

"Believe me, I know how lucky I am."

Kasey and Duncan shook hands with Justice. "Thanks, man. We really appreciate it," Kasey said.

Duncan wrapped his arm around Julia's shoulder. "So you ready to go home and show off your ring to Kat, or do we still need to go furniture shopping?"

Julia patted his cheek and laughed. "Oh honey, just because you put a ring on it doesn't mean you get out of shopping for a new coffee table."

"That's what I was afraid of," he mumbled.

Kasey pulled them both against his large chest and kissed Julia on the cheek. "And we wouldn't have it any other way. Let's go shopping."

THE END

For upcoming releases, exclusive content, contests and give-aways, be sure to Subscribe to my newsletter Plus as a newsletter subscriber you'll get access to a newsletter sub-scriber-only FREE book.

Continue reading for a sneak peek at Everything to Me . The first book in the Playing for Keeps Series. If you love sports romance check it out!

Excerpt from
Everything to Me

Holy cow, this was really happening. Today was the day she was finally going to get Pete Saunders out of her system once and for all. The man had been living in her head rent free for too long.

Kendall's hands trembled as she knocked on Pete's front door. Shifting her carry-on bag up her shoulder while she waited for him to answer, she mentally prepared herself for seeing him again. Taking a deep breath, she exhaled, trying to calm her nerves. Oh boy. She couldn't believe she was staying at Pete's house, or that he'd agreed. When her brother, Ryan, had suggested she stay with his best friend while she was in town, she'd thought he was crazy. But the more she'd thought about it, the more it seemed like the perfect way to finally get over this stupid adolescent crush. Well, here's hoping the reality lives up to her vivid imagination.

The front door opened and her teenage crush stood before her, in the flesh, and even better than she remembered. The air whooshed out of her lungs at the first sight of him in his low-slung, gray sweatpants and threadbare Metallica t-shirt. She thought she'd been prepared. Clearly, she wasn't. What was it about this man that he always affected her like this?

Pete stared back at her, not saying anything, and she shifted nervously on her feet. "Hey. Sorry, I'm late. There were some issues with the plane."

"No problem," he replied. His green eyes scanned down her body, lingering on her waist, then back up. She licked her lips. Pete had never looked at her like this before. Like she was a woman and not just his friend's annoying little sister. Damn, it was a heady feeling.

She stepped forward and wrapped her arms around him. "Hi, thanks for letting me stay."

"Of course." He stepped back and looked down at her. "It's good to see you, Peanut."

And they were back. Whatever that brief look had been, it was gone. Now she was just Ryan's kid sister, Peanut.

"Can we not call me that? Please."

Pete's eyes twinkled as he smirked at her. "What? You don't like the nickname?" He chucked her on the chin. "It's cute 'cuz you're so little."

"I'm not that small," she grumbled.

Pete raised his eyebrow. "You're not very big."

She placed her hands on her hips and glared at him. "Next to you? No. But I'm 5ft4. That's average, I'll have you know."

He chuckled and raised his hands up in defeat. "Sorry, my mistake."

She stepped past him and walked into the entranceway. Her eyes were drawn to the exposed brick and wood beams. His place was beautiful, so warm and inviting. When she'd first pulled up to the older building, she'd expected some modern converted warehouse with lots of metal and white. But this was anything but that. "Wow," she murmured.

Pete smiled. "Come on in."

A calico cat popped out from behind the entranceway bench and wove its way around her legs. "Well, hello there. And who are you?" Kendall said as she bent down to scratch the fur behind the cat's ears.

"That's Mooch," Pete replied.

"Mooch? Seriously?"

"Yeah, it fits him perfectly. He looks all cute and innocent, but he's not. He's crafty." Pete narrowed his eyes as he looked at the cat in question.

"When did you get a cat? I thought you hated them." The boy she remembered had sided with Ryan to convince her parents not to allow her to get a cat when she was 15 because they smelled and were gross. Never in a million years would she have pictured him with one of his own.

"I do, but—" He bent down and scooped up Mooch. "He's not really mine."

"Oh no?" She eyed the cat tree in the corner of the room. "He looks like he's your cat."

"He's not. He's just recovering from an injury and needed a place to crash." He stroked his hand along the back flank of the cat and she saw the injury to his hind leg.

Kendall bit her cheek to hold in her laugh at his serious tone. "Gotcha, he's just a temporary roommate, then?" She walked closer to examine the stitches. "How'd he get hurt?" she asked.

"The vet wasn't sure, but thought maybe he'd been in a fight."

"The vet?" She smirked, then coughed to hide her amusement. "So, you took the cat that isn't yours to the vet?"

"Well..." Pete's ears turned red as he looked down at the ground. "He was hurt." He rubbed the back of his neck, his bicep flexing with the movement. "I couldn't just leave him."

She stroked the cat's ear and glanced up at Pete. Her heartbeat quickened the way it always did when she was close to her brother's good friend. He even smelled good. "How did you know he was hurt?"

He shrugged. "He came over to show me?"

Kendall snorted. "What do you mean, he came over to show you?"

Pete glanced at her and scowled. "He's been hanging around lately and he showed up yesterday morning and he looked pretty rough, so I took him to the vet. They had to put a drain in his leg so it doesn't get infected, and I couldn't just put him back on the street when it will need to be taken out in a few days."

"Of course not. So, you got a cat."

"No, it's just temporary." Pete scowled.

"And the cat tree?" she asked, indicating the elaborate tree in the corner.

"I didn't want him to get bored," Pete muttered.

Oh my god, could the man be any sweeter? She patted him on the shoulder. "I hate to break it to you, but I think you've got yourself a cat."

He glanced down at the cat in his arms. "Shit."

Kendall laughed. "All right, show me around this ridiculous place of yours." She looked at the high warehouse ceilings in the living room and over to the wooden staircase that led to what looked like additional rooms upstairs. "How did you find this place?" She trailed her hand along the smooth kitchen countertop. The kitchen was a cook's dream. She traced the lines in the quartz that made it look like marble. It was exactly the counters she would have chosen if she had her own home.

"You don't like it?" Pete asked.

"What? No, I love it, it's amazing."

"Oh, you said ridiculous, so I wasn't sure."

She squeezed his arm at the hint of vulnerability she heard in his voice. "I meant ridiculous in a good way."

Pete grinned, exposing his perfect white teeth. Her heart fluttered in her chest. It was no wonder he had all kinds of product endorsements. The man was gorgeous.

"Your brother thought I was an idiot when I bought this place."

"Yeah, well, my brother has no vision." She looked around the open floor plan of the warehouse. "Does this go right out to water?" She dashed towards the large sliding glass doors along the back wall.

"Yeah. I've got a dock with my boat right outside. It's perfect."

She looked at the wall of glass along the entire side of the space. "What about privacy?" she asked, pointing at the windows.

"One way glass. I can see out, but no one can see in."

"Oh, that's genius," she replied.

Pete waggled his eyebrows. "I'm not just a pretty face."

"Well, smart enough to buy a cool place when you see one," she teased.

"No, this was just a huge abandoned old warehouse when I bought it. That's why your brother thought I was nuts to want to live here. I had it converted into three separate units. I sold the other two, which paid for mine."

"Seriously?" She looked around the space with fresh eyes. Seeing everything about the place differently now that she knew Pete had a hand in creating the entire place. "I didn't know you knew how to do this kind of stuff."

He laughed. "I don't, but I'm smart enough to hire people who can build it the way I want."

"But you picked out everything and designed it?"

His face turned red and he shrugged. "I know what I like, so it's not that hard to hire people to do it when you have money."

"Do you have pictures of it from before?"

"Yeah." He grabbed her hand. Excitement zipped through her veins at the simple contact. Good lord, she really was like a schoolgirl around him. "Come here," he said as he tugged her towards a door on the left that led into a huge home gym. He stopped in front of a row of large, framed photographs of an old, rundown and grungy warehouse.

She leaned in closer to look at the pictures. "Is this it?" She trailed her fingers along the photo. It looked nothing like the place now. "Wow, Pete. This is amazing. I don't know how you looked at that and made this."

He laughed. "Again, I didn't make it. I hired people to make it." He looked around the room. "Well, this is clearly the gym. Feel free to use it while you are here." He glanced back at her. "You never said how long you were here for."

"I think I'll be here a week. I hope that's okay."

"Yeah, of course it's fine. You can stay as long as you need to," he told her.

They walked back out into the main living area, and Pete gestured to the stairs along the right side of the room. "Bedrooms are upstairs." He gestured for her to go first.

"Are you helping Ryan with his renos, because he'd be an idiot not to have asked your opinion after seeing this place?"

"Yeah, I helped him with a few things. We have pretty different taste."

Kendall snorted. That was putting it mildly. Her big brother was a traditionalist. Ever since he was a little boy and talked about making it to the major leagues, he'd dreamed of having a big house with a gate that he needed to buzz people into and the house had to have a pool. When he'd finally bought his first home, those things had still been on the top of the list. "I have to admit, I thought I was a bit more traditional too, but now that I've seen this place, I think you've converted me."

A smile split across Pete's face. "Yeah?"

"Oh my god, yes. Now show me the bedroom."

Silence filled the room. She glanced over at him and the air crackled between them. He stared at her, then cleared his throat and the moment was gone. "Right, I'll show you to your room."

What had that been about? She'd had a crush on Pete since the first time she'd laid eyes on him when she was twelve years old and it had never gone away. If anything, over the years, her crush had grown. Now, being here in his space. Seeing what he created and getting this inside glimpse of the man he'd become. The crush would never go away. She'd always just assumed she didn't stand a chance, but if that look was anything to go by, maybe she did.

Conscious of Pete walking up the stairs behind her, she slowed down slightly and added a little extra sway to her hips. She heard him groan behind her.

"What was that?" she asked.

"Nothing. I just noticed the cat's toy is leaning against the built-in vacuum vent and I don't want to forget to move it before I turn it on."

"Gotcha." She smirked and flipped her brown hair over her shoulder. Seducing Pete Saunders just became her new mission while she was here. If he was interested in her in the least, there was no way she wasn't making the most of this trip.

At the top of the stairs, Pete brushed past her and walked into a large bedroom. A king-sized bed sat in the center of the room. Large windows looked out over the harbor. "One way glass in here too?" she asked.

"Of course." He picked up a remote from the bedside table. "You can add some extra tint to the windows as well if you don't like the sun beaming in. It's kind of like built-in blinds, but it's just a window filter." He set the remote down on the table. "I like being woken up to the morning sun, but I know not everyone does." He continued to walk deeper into the bedroom. "You have your own bathroom through here," he said, and led her through the doorway.

"Wow. This bathroom alone is as big as my bedroom at home." She eyed up the steam shower with multiple heads and moaned. "Oh, I'm going to enjoy using that."

Pete cleared his throat. "Right, uh...um...make yourself at home. The towels on the rack are clean." He glanced at her, then back at the shower. "I'll um...I'll let you get settled."

"Uh-uh, I want to see your room," she replied.

Pete groaned. "Sure."

"What's the groan about?" she asked.

"Nothing. I didn't groan."

"Yeah, you did."

"Jesus, Ken, drop it, please."

She stepped closer to him, and he stepped back. "Do I make you uncomfortable, Pete?" she asked.

"What? No, of course not."

Interesting. Then why did he look like he wanted to flee? She took another step toward him. His eyes darkened as he held her stare. "You sure?" she whispered.

"Be careful, Kendall."

"Of what?"

"What you're asking for," he replied. His nostrils flared as he watched her.

She placed her hand against his muscular chest. "What am I asking for?" she licked her lips as she held his stare.

"Fuck," he muttered and stepped away from her. "That's a bad idea, Kendall, and you know it."

"Why is it a bad idea?"

"Because your brother would kill me," Pete protested.

"No, he wouldn't. You guys are friends. He likes you."

Pete rolled his eyes. "There's a big difference between liking me as a buddy and liking me enough to let me touch his sister. Ryan doesn't like anyone that much."

"Well then, it's a good thing my brother doesn't get to decide who I fuck."

"Jesus," Pete groaned.

"In case you hadn't noticed. I'm all grown-up, Pete."

"Believe me, I noticed," he grumbled.

"So, what's the problem?" she asked and stepped toward him again. "We're obviously attracted to each other. We're both healthy, single adults. What's the harm in having a little fun while I'm here?"

"Again, your brother is one of my best friends and he'd kill me if I took advantage of you while you're staying with me."

"Oh my god, did you seriously just say that?" Kendall scoffed. "Take advantage of me, because the poor little lady couldn't possibly know her own mind." She poked him in the chest. "Believe me, Pete. I know my own mind and if I fuck a guy, it's because I want to fuck him. Not because I'm so naïve he's tricked me into it."

He caught her hand as she continued to poke his chest. "I didn't mean it like that," he growled. "There's just like a code that you don't cross. You don't fuck your friend's ex, and you sure as hell keep your hands off his sister."

"But what if the sister wants you to put your hands on her?" She leaned in so their bodies were touching and he sucked in a breath.

"Still, he'd kill me if he found out."

"So maybe he doesn't need to find out," she whispered as she leaned in closer and shifted her hips. She could feel him getting hard against her stomach. He was definitely not immune to her. "I'm only here for a week, Pete. My brother is out of town. You and I barely ever see each other." She leaned in and whispered in his ear. "No one would ever have to know."

His hand curled around her hip and she bit back a smile. Not wanting to press her luck, she stepped back. "Think about it," she said and turned and walked out of the bathroom.

His body tensed like a caged animal and he looked around the room. "We should head back downstairs," he said.

"Sure."

Pete started to push past her. When his chest brushed against her shoulder, he stopped, muttered something unintelligible, and gestured for her to go first. Kendall bit back a smile. It was like he was scared to touch her. Maybe this would be easier than she thought.

About the Author

Lauren Fraser resides in British Columbia, Canada, with her husband, two children, and two dogs. When she's not busy writing, Lauren loves to spend time with her family outside—camping, hiking and paddle boarding.

Lauren writes about love and relationships in many different forms, but in the end, she's a sucker for a happy ending. She is multi-published and loves to hear from her readers. For the latest updates, visit her website.

Website http://www.laurenfraser.com/
Newsletter: http://www.laurenfraser.com/newsletter

ALSO BY LAUREN FRASER

Stand Alone Books

Letting Go

The Geek Next Door

Dani's Duo

Longing for Kayla

Too Hot

Sex, Sin and Surf

Aged to Perfection

Yielding for Him